SHEARER

LAND-
LUBBERS

LAND-LUBBERS

Hodder Children's Books

a division of Hachette Children's Books

A Catalogue record for this book is available
from the British Library

ISBN-13: 978 0 340 90229 5

Typeset in New Baskerville by Avon DataSet Ltd,
Bidford on Avon, Warwickshire

Printed and bound in Great Britain by
Bookmarque Ltd, Croydon, Surrey

The paper and board used in this paperback by
Hodder Children's Books are natural recyclable products made from
wood grown in sustainable forests. The manufacturing processes
conform to the environmental regulations
of the country of origin.

Hodder Children's Books
a division of Hachette Children's Books
338 Euston Road
London NW1 3BH

LANDLUBBERS

I guess, looking back now, that we had already started to take things too much for granted – all the luxury, and the room service, and the five star comforts and the swimming pool and the steam room. I loved that steam room. You could sit in there, slowly poaching, as if you were lost in the middle of a warm, damp fog.

Yes, it's amazing how quickly you get used to things, to high-living and to taking everything for granted. You think it's just going to go on for ever and never stop. It never crosses your mind that you could suddenly lose it all, in a matter of moments. No, you just go on sleepwalking through this cosseted and pampered, candyfloss world of luxury, where there aren't any sharp edges to hurt you at all.

And then suddenly you bump into something unexpected, and you get a rude awakening.

1

Us

It doesn't really matter if you've never heard of Clive before as he can be easily summed up in a few words. The words which mostly apply to Clive are 'case' and 'nut', 'big' and 'head', or 'wit' and 'half' – though not necessarily in that order.

Although Clive and I were born at the same time, we are not identical twins – I am relieved to say. When it comes to good looks, Clive got the short straw and I got the long one. Not that Clive actually looks like a short straw as he is too fat for that. Clive looks more like the slimy stuff which aliens leave behind them in science fiction films – the stuff that nobody wants to step in.

For ages Clive thought that I was five minutes older than him, and he resented me for it. He said that I had got him with my elbow and had stopped him being born first. However, the midwife from the maternity hospital turned up one day to say that she had made a mistake and that Clive was actually the oldest after all, which chuffed him up no end.

However, Clive does not have the mental equipment to be the oldest, and on top of that, it is too late for him to be the oldest anyway as it is already written down on the birth certificates that I am five minutes older than him, and birth certificates cannot be changed – at least not unless you have a certificate saying that you can change your certificate and Clive doesn't have that.

Clive is not the sort of person to whom anyone would ever give a certificate – unless it was to say that he is a certified loony.

Therefore, no matter what Clive says, I am still the eldest, in that I am sensible and level-headed, whereas Clive is nothing but a glue-head with a tin of spaghetti where his brains ought to be. Being the eldest does bring many worries and responsibilities with it, but I just have to shoulder these as best I can. I did let Clive have a go at making all the decisions for a little while but he couldn't even make one. In fact he almost starved to death, unable to make up his mind between the Rice Krispies and Cornflakes at breakfast. If I hadn't told him to have muesli, he'd still be standing there now with confusion in his eyes and his spoon in his hand, wondering what to do for the best while the milk went off.

Clive and I don't have a mum, which is the sad part. She died when we were young and although I never say as much, I have to be Clive's mum as well as his brother, which means that I have to make him eat his vegetables even when he doesn't want to, as they are good for him.

Sometimes I manage to make him eat my vegetables as well. He was not very keen to do this at first but I had to explain to him that it was only eating double vegetables that would kill off his tapeworms. Clive said that he did not know that he had any tapeworms, which I said he had probably got from eating chocolate. I had to explain to him that eating chocolate was always a risky business and that people who did too much of it could end up with a great, big, six-foot long worm living inside them and the only way to get rid of it was by eating extra vegetables.

Clive got a bit worried then and so when I offered to swap my vegetables for his chocolate he snapped up the offer straight away.

'But aren't you worried about getting a big worm yourself?' he said.

'I'll risk it for your sake, Clive,' I said. 'Anything for you.'

So, for the next three weeks he ate all my vegetables and I had all his chocolate. Then I explained stage two of the cure to him. 'Clive,' I said, 'a diet of double vegetables weakens tapeworms, but to finish them off properly, there's only one thing to do.'

'What's that?' Clive asked.

'Hit yourself over the head with a brick,' I explained.

'Hard?' Clive said.

'Very hard,' I said, and I went off to get him a brick from the garden, where Dad was building a patio. 'There you are, Clive,' I said. 'Just hit yourself over the head with that a couple of times, and when you wake up, your worms will have vanished completely. You just have to stun them a bit so that they get dizzy and then they crawl out of your ears and slither off to die in the garden.'

So Clive was just about to give himself a good, solid whack on the head with the nice brick I had found him when Dad walked into the kitchen and asked what was going on.

When Clive explained that I had suggested he cure himself of tapeworms with a spot of brick therapy, Dad got a bit angry and said he'd never heard the like of it and we both ought to know better, but I said that as Clive was the eldest, or liked to think he was, it was all down to him and I couldn't be expected to know any better as I was only little.

After Clive found out that he didn't have a big worm living in his head he said that he was going to get his own back on me somehow and that he was going to go back to eating chocolate big time. I had to tell him then that I would go careful if I was him as there was still the poltergeist living in his underpants to worry about. Clive got into a panic then and started running about the house yelling, 'My pants are haunted! I've got a ghost in my pants!' But Dad told him to pack it in as he was trying to watch the sport on the telly, and when did he ever get a chance to have a minute to himself, he'd like to know.

Although there is only me and Clive and Dad in the house (mostly) we are all quite domesticated and know how to use the washing machine, the cooker, the tumble drier and the dishwasher, and even the iron. We also know how to plug in the vacuum cleaner and how to turn it on as well.

Our expertise in these areas often amazes people, especially friends of Dad – who are usually ladies. Dad has had several lady friends over the years, sometimes they get tired and have to stay the night as they are too exhausted to go home. Dad has a friend who is not a lady, who he used to be in the navy with years ago. Sometimes he comes round and they sit and drink beer. This is Kenny. He has a parrot and an earring. He wears the earring in his left ear, though he leaves the parrot at home.

'Never thought of marrying again?' I overheard Kenny ask Dad one night.

'I have, Kenny,' Dad said. 'Many a time. But who'd

take on those two? I mean, it always starts off all right. We get friendly, I bring her round, she meets them, they're on their best behaviour, it's all going well . . .'

'And then?' Kenny said.

'Then it all goes pear-shaped.'

'How come?'

'Oh, you name it – bricks, or six-foot tapeworms, or haunted underwear, or who's the eldest, or something like that. The riot starts and she's off.'

'Pity,' Kenny said.

'Yes,' Dad said.

'Boys need a mother,' Kenny said.

'They do,' Dad agreed. 'But it's not every woman who wants to take on a ready-made family – especially one with haunted underpants.'

'Let's have another beer,' Kenny said.

'Yes,' Dad said. 'Why not?'

When I overheard conversations like that, I would feel a bit sorry for Dad and felt it was a shame that Clive's appalling behaviour was stopping Dad from getting married again. It was hard for Dad, but at least he had us to console him and to stop him from getting lonely, and we had him too. So we weren't unhappy. We just had a bit missing – our mum – but we tried to fill the gap as best we could, even though we knew that we never could really and that there would always be a gap for ever, and even if Dad found us a new mum, she would never be our old one, no matter how nice she was. But that was life and you just had to face it, no matter how old or young you were. Life doesn't make any allowances, not for adults or for children either.

After the navy, Dad worked on cruise ships for years. He ended up as Chief Steward, which was pretty good, but Clive and I missed him when he was away as we had to go and stay with our grandparents. Grandma and Granddad are both very nice although they do tend to sleep a lot, especially Granddad, who has special corduroy trousers for doing his sleeping in. They more or less double up as pyjamas.

Granddad claims that he just 'has a nap' or is 'off for a snooze' or he might 'close his eyes for five minutes'. But as far as I can tell he is napping about five hours a day. The rest of the time he is in the garden, which he is very proud of. Clive reckons that he goes out and polishes the grass when nobody is looking.

When Granddad bends over his rose bushes, his corduroy trousers make an almost irresistible target, and it is at moments like this that you wish you had brought a catapult or a small bow and arrow or a hammer and a large cork.

One time Clive and I got so fed up with being shunted off to Grandma's that we decided to accompany Dad on one of his cruise ships. We managed to stow away and had a great time until

Clive gave the game away, but fortunately I saved the day when the ship was hijacked by robbers.

You may possibly even have heard about this, as I jotted down the facts and particulars in my notebook and I even showed it around afterwards to a few people.

Anyway, Dad gave up the ships after that, and ran a restaurant for a while which was financed by Mrs Dominics, one of his regular passengers, who was ever so rich and had got friendly with us.

Although Mrs Dominics was a very clean person, she was also filthy rich. I asked Dad to explain about being clean and filthy at the same time. He said that this is known as a paradox. I didn't like to say that I didn't know what a paradox was so I made out that I did. When I mentioned it to Clive later, he said that a paradox is a kind of parrot, a bit like that one that Dad's friend Kenny has, only it doesn't make such a mess on your shoulder.

Anyway again, the long and the short of it – as well as the wide and the broad of it – was that Mrs Dominics found herself in a spot of trouble, and who else could she turn to in her moment of need than yours truly, me and Clive and Dad. We had seen her out of tight spots before, back in our cruise liner days, so it was only natural that she should turn to us when the spots started tightening once again.

Clive says that there is nothing worse than a tight spot, and he should know, as he has had loads of them – spots that is. Clive has had all sorts of spots in his time, not just tight ones, but big, gloopy ones too, the size of fried eggs. The trouble with Clive and his spots is that he won't leave them alone. I told him he should, but he said he would leave the spots alone when they left him alone, but not until.

Well, there we all were one afternoon, round in the manager's office at The Stowaway restaurant when Mrs Dominics drove up in her chauffeured limousine with Chaswick at the wheel, to see how business was doing. Mrs Dominics has a big old car called a Rolls Royce, and Chaswick, who drives it, has a grey suit and a flat cap, which he never takes off. Clive says that this is because he has a flat head as well and is embarrassed about it.

While Dad and Mrs Dominics chatted in the office and went through the menus and the accounts, Clive and I went outside to have a look at the car and at Chaswick.

'Can we sit in the back?' Clive asked him.

'No,' he said. 'Clear off. You're too grubby and sticky-looking.'

This was not an exaggeration on Chaswick's part, for Clive is very sticky-looking sometimes, especially after meals. Clive is so sticky-looking that if you picked him up and threw him against a window, or another smooth surface of that nature, he would probably stay there and not slide down at all. In fact, in many ways, Clive is like a rubber sucker.

'Mrs Dominics said we could sit in the car,' Clive told Chaswick.

'No, she didn't,' Chaswick said.

'Yes, she did,' Clive insisted – as he has no qualms about lying, though he will tell the truth sometimes if it is a matter of life and death (his usually).

'She said that we could sit in the back of the car and that you were to drive us round the town and call us "sir" and "young master" and take us for large ice-creams which, as a special favour, we're to let you pay for.'

'She said no such thing,' Chaswick said. 'And if she did, I want it in writing. If you think I'm letting you muck this car up from the inside out, you've got another think coming. Now buzz off before I adjust your head with the tyre lever.'

We could tell that Chaswick was not in a very good mood that day and that he had probably got out of the wrong side of his basket in the morning, so we left him to his car and his flat cap and went back into the restaurant to see if Dad and Mrs Dominics had finished talking.

It was always a good idea to be hanging about when Mrs Dominics left, for when she saw me and Clive, she would give us a big smile and say, 'Well, there you are, boys! A sight for sore eyes and a breath of fresh air as always.' (This was not strictly true in Clive's case, however, as Clive is not a breath of fresh air by any stretch. Clive is more like toxic waste. In fact one day at school Clive got a bad stomach during the geography lesson and as a result they had to evacuate the classroom. Three pupils were carried out on stretchers and a fireman wearing breathing apparatus had to go back in for the class gerbil, which had passed out in its treadmill and was lying there with its little feet pointing upwards.)

Anyway, once Mrs Dominics had spotted us, she would reach for her pocketbook, and while Dad said things like, 'No, no, Mrs Dominics, you mustn't really . . . you're far too generous . . . you spoil those two . . .' she would peel a few notes off from her wodge of cash and hand a couple to Clive and a few to me and say, 'There you are, boys, treat yourselves to a little something.'

So I would then say, 'Oh really, Mrs Dominics, we couldn't possibly . . .' while Clive all but grabbed the money out of her hand. Then Dad would say, 'And what do you say, boys?' And we would say, 'Thank you very much, Mrs Dominics, very kind of you indeed.' And then she would say, 'Oh, it's my pleasure, boys, you're more than welcome. What use is money if you can't spread it around?' And Dad would then discreetly clamp his hand over Clive's mouth to stop him saying, 'You can spread a bit more around if you like then – you can spread a big heap of it in my direction.'

And then we would see her to the car, and wave

goodbye as she motored off in her Rolls Royce with Chaswick at the wheel, driving off with his natty driving gloves on his hands and his flat cap on his head.

On this day though, it didn't happen. No 'There you are, boys!' No 'Sight for sore eyes.' No 'Breath of fresh air.' And worst of all – no money! Mrs Dominics hardly seemed to notice us. She just gave us a vague, preoccupied smile, and she turned to Dad and said, 'You'll think that over then, will you, John? And you'll let me know? As soon as possible?'

'Of course, Mrs Dominics. Yes, I will.'

'Would you be able to decide by tomorrow evening?'

'Yes, I think so.'

'OK. I shall call you then.'

And off she went, without so much as a fiver between us, and she purred away in the big car, looking worried and troubled.

'Is Mrs Dominics all right, Dad?' Clive asked when she had gone. 'I think she must be very ill.'

'What makes you say that, Clive?' Dad asked.

'She never gave me any money,' Clive said. 'I think her mind must be going.'

'Quite the contrary,' Dad said. 'I would have thought that not giving you any money was a sign of robust mental health.'

But Clive didn't really understand that. And, to be honest, neither did I.

'So what did she want, Dad?' I asked. 'What did she want you to decide about? Is it important stuff? Are there adventures in it? Is there travel involved and new sights and unfamiliar places? Does it involve going back to sea and seeing the world and watching the sun go down on distant horizons and large cooked breakfasts and that kind of thing?'

Dad looked thoughtful.

'No, it's not exactly that,' he said. 'Though it would involve a change of scenery, and new sights, and a new home for a while, and fresh challenges and new and demanding responsibilities . . .'

'And adventures?' Clive said hopefully. 'Any of them?'

Dad gave him a look, as if adventures weren't the important thing, and were really only a secondary issue.

'Eh, possibly, Clive,' he said. 'You never can tell. Possibly.'

'Then I think we should do it then,' Clive said. And, reluctant as I am ever to agree with Clive on anything at all, I just had to nod my head.

'Yes, I think we should do it too, Dad,' I said. 'That's what I think.'

But, 'Hold on a second,' Dad said. 'Aren't you two jumping the gun a bit? I haven't even told you what it is yet.'

Only somehow, that didn't really seem to matter. Because you can't be fussy when it comes to adventures. There's no sense in being picky about them. You just have to take what comes along, and make the most of it. For you never know how long you'll have to wait for the next one. In fact, one might never come along again.

Then Dad dropped the big bombshell.

'You see,' he said. 'When I mentioned fresh challenges and new responsibilities and new horizons, I really meant for myself – not you two.'

'You m-mean,' Clive stuttered, 'th-that we wouldn't be c-coming with you?'

'Sorry, Clive,' Dad said. 'No.'

'Then what would happen to us, Dad? Where would we go? What would become of us?'

'Well, that wouldn't be a problem at all,' Dad said. 'If I decide to take this opportunity up – not that I have yet – but if I do, well, you can both go and live at Granddad's.'

'Granddad's? Granddad's!'

'It would only be for a couple of months.'

'Months . . . months . . . ahhh . . .'

I just managed to catch Clive as he fainted. Then, as I was holding him up, I thought, what am I bothering doing this for? So I let him slide down to the floor, where he belonged.

I could tell from looking at him as he lay there, that if nothing else worked out, and he failed all his exams, he still had a good career ahead of him as a carpet, or possibly a small rug.

He certainly needed vacuuming. In fact once someone had run the hoover over him, he'd have made a very nice doormat.

I thought I might wipe my feet on him, just to try him out. But Dad looked stern and said that I wasn't to do it. On reflection I could see that this was probably right. There was no sense in wiping my feet on Clive as I would only have got my shoes dirty.

2

Rejects

'Two months!'

Even Granddad's old corduroy trousers had gone pale.

'Well, not two months exactly,' Dad explained. 'More six weeks, really. Just for the duration of the summer holidays.'

Grandma's teacup rattled against the saucer as she put it down. For some strange reason, her hands were trembling. I put it down to the weather and old age.

'You want us to have both of them – Clive as well – for six weeks. Here? With us? Poor, defenceless pensioners?'

Dad looked hurt and pained.

'You mean,' he said, 'you wouldn't want them? Your own grandchildren?'

Grandma poured herself out another stiff cup of

tea. I noticed she put five sugars in it, which was unusual for her. All she normally had was half an artificial sweetener.

'No, we'd love to have them – love to, John, dear. Of course we would. Wouldn't we, Hubert?'

She looked across the sitting room towards Granddad, who was having one of his asthma attacks and trying to find his inhaler.

'Ahhhh . . .' Granddad wheezed. 'Love to haaaave them. Course we would. Only . . .'

There was always an 'only' these days. It hadn't always been like that. When Clive and I had been little, Grandma and Granddad had never wanted us to leave or to go home. Of course, that had been back in the days when even Clive had been a little bit cute – hard as it is to believe now. But those days had long gone.

Short stays were fine, and they always made us welcome, but anything over a few days and Granddad would be going round with his blood-pressure monitor clamped to his arm, swallowing pills while staring at the digital read-out and saying things like, 'It's up to three hundred and fifty over two hundred and ninety-one now. I don't think I can hold out much longer. How in God's name did he get a tortoise to climb to the top of the monkey puzzle tree and get stuck there!'

Grandma would also be OK for a couple of days, but then she would start to get her allergies again, or she would sit in front of the TV with her knitting, muttering things like, 'And they used to be such lovely little boys too. Whatever happened? Whatever happened? Oh dear, oh dear.'

Anyway, there we all were, me and Clive and Dad and Granddad and Grandma, all there in the sitting room, with me and Clive on the sofa and Granddad parked up inside his corduroy trousers with the expanding waistband for when he got bigger. We all looked pretty gloomy.

The truth was, you see, that six weeks at Granddad's was no treat and no bed of roses for us either. Maybe Clive and I had got a bit too lively for Grandma and Granddad as the years had gone by, but from our point of view, they seemed to have slowed down so much they'd all but ground to a halt.

Once we'd had a great time round there, but now we'd developed something of a generation gap. Two days of each other's company was fine, anything more than that was disaster, as they got exhausted and Clive got more and more bored – which always spelt trouble.

We all sat and sipped our tea – apart from Clive, who slurped his orange juice. I glanced at him from the corners of my eyes and noticed that he was trying to drink it through his nose again. But I didn't say anything. I thought I'd leave it to the adults.

'The thing is, John, dear,' Grandma was saying,

'that when Alison' – Alison was our mum's name –'
when Alison so sadly . . .'

Grandma glanced at Clive. She had to be careful
what she said. Clive is unpredictable when it comes
to memories of Mum. Sometimes he's fine. Other
times, someone just has to mention her name and
he's inconsolable.

Anyway, Grandma got away with it that time. Clive
just looked at her sadly, but he didn't say anything,
or give way to his emotions.

'. . . when Alison so sadly . . .'

'I know,' Dad said. 'I know.'

'Well, when she did, John,' Grandma continued,
'we were more than happy to help in any way we
could, and to have the boys as much as possible,
only now . . .'

She didn't need to say it, really. But she said
it anyway.

'Only now – we're getting old. And well, growing
boys can be such a handful, and while I'm sure we
could cope for a few days, or even a week or two –
a whole six weeks . . .'

'Six weeks . . .' Granddad echoed in a pathetic
sort of tone. 'Six weeks!'

'And besides,' Gran added, 'we were thinking of
going to Spain.'

Clive brightened up at that and stopped trying to
blow his nose on the sofa.

'Spain!' he said. 'Great! I love Spain!'

'You've never been there,' I reminded him.

'That's why I love it,' he said. 'It's somewhere new. I can't wait to go to Spain. I'll be able to practise my French.'

Grandma's teacup was rattling again and Granddad was having a fresh squirt on his asthma inhaler. I think it was the thought of taking Clive to Spain that had done it. At their age it would have been on a par with going travelling in the company of a python.

'I'm afraid,' Grandma said (though you could tell she was more relieved than worried), 'that the place we were thinking of going to is only for retired people. You have to be over sixty to stay there – otherwise we'd love to take you with us, of course.' Then she turned to Dad. 'So you see, John, dear,' she said, 'it would be rather difficult for us. I mean, we'd love to have them for a week or two, to help you out – but for the whole summer holiday . . .'

Then she let the rest of it trail off, as if it were best left implied, but unsaid, as it was just as clear that way, if not clearer.

If Dad felt disappointed and let down, he didn't let it show. But then, he had to see it from Gran and Granddad's point of view. They were getting on, and Clive was a handful. More than a handful. A cageful if anything. And it wasn't that they had refused outright – just not for a whole six weeks.

'OK, boys,' Dad said. 'Let's make a move.'

21

So we did.

We said goodbye to Grandma and Granddad and we left and we walked back home. We hadn't come in the car as Dad had wanted to stretch his legs, so we had to stretch ours along with him.

We were all a bit quiet as we walked on home. Finally Clive broke the silence.

'Nobody wants us, do they, Dad? Nobody.'

Dad looked at him and smiled.

'Course they do, Clive,' he said. 'Come on. Don't worry. Let's stop off at the shop on our way and get some oven chips to have with our tea.'

'All right then,' Clive said. 'Good idea.'

He brightened up instantly. But that's Clive for you. He's not what you call the complicated sort. A bag of chips, a packet of chewing gum, and that's him distracted. He's not the deep and sensitive type like me – even though he does claim to be the eldest.

I went on brooding. It was right what he had said. Nobody did want us. At least not all of us, not together. There had been ladies who had wanted Dad, but they hadn't wanted Clive and me into the bargain.

Mum had wanted us though. She had wanted us all. But she was gone and would never come back. But she had loved us, warts and everything. And that took quite some doing in Clive's case, as he has a lot of warts to love.

'What'll we do, Dad? What'll we do now?' I asked.

Dad gave me one of his chin-up, not-to-worry, we'll-survive looks.

'It'll be OK,' he said. 'I'll just have to tell Mrs Dominics that I can't take her offer up and we'll just go on as we are.'

We walked a few steps.

'Was it a good offer, Dad?' I said.

'Yes,' he said. 'It was.'

Clive had wandered off ahead of us. He had stopped by a low wall, where he was trying to hypnotize a pigeon.

'Was it something you really wanted to do, Dad?' I said.

He said, 'Oh, not that much. I wasn't bothered.' But I could tell that wasn't true. 'I'll give her a call later,' he said, 'and explain the situation.'

I felt worse then ever then, for not only did nobody want us, we were holding Dad back too, and stopping him doing what he wanted to, and making him turn his back on big opportunities.

It was all Clive's fault. I would have told him so too. Only when I caught up with him, he looked a bit glassy-eyed and far away.

I think the pigeon had hypnotized him.

3

Sausages and Sweets

When Clive had been the youngest, all he had wanted to do was to be the eldest and to be in charge and boss people about, but now he was the eldest, he didn't know what to do next. The responsibility was all too much for him. Clive is not a natural leader like I am, and he was reduced to saying things like, 'Let's all pull together now,' and 'OK now, let's look lively!' and meaningless stuff like that.

The truth is that Clive had no more idea of how to look lively than a three-toed sloth. I have seen livelier pebbles than Clive, and I even had a pet rock once, called Montmorency, and he was twice as lively as Clive will ever be. In fact there are lots of dead things in the cemetery that are livelier than Clive – even vampires, who, although they sleep all day, do at least have the decency to get up at night and put a day's work in then. But Clive could not even make it as a vampire, as he wouldn't even bother to get up in the evenings. In fact, if Clive was a vampire (and I'm not saying he isn't; he might well be for all I know, because I don't keep an eye on him all the time) he would be the sort of vampire who just lay there in his coffin waiting for one of the other vampires to get up and put the kettle on. Being so idle and lacking motivation is the reason why Clive is a fat bum and why he will never really make it as an elder brother – no matter what it does or doesn't say on any birth certificates.

The strange thing, though, is that although I had thought for years how nice it must be to be the younger one and not have to shoulder any responsibilities and such, now that I *was* the youngest, it wasn't as much fun as I had anticipated.

I could see that for someone like Clive, who is at heart an irresponsible half-wit with a brain the size of a small piece of sweetcorn (and probably the same colour), being the youngest was a doddle. For Clive was an expert at messing things up and making five out of two and two, but for more serious, intellectual types, like myself, being the youngest was turning out to be a waste of my time and talents.

I decided to put this to Clive one morning, so I got him on his own when Dad was out in the garden reading the instructions on his slug pellets.

'Now see here, young Clive,' I said. But he bristled immediately, as I might have expected.

'What do you mean "young"?' he said. 'It's "old and venerable" Clive to you, young whippersnapper. The midwife came round from the hospital, don't forget, and she confessed there had been a mix-up and in fact I'd been born first and was two minutes older than you. So let's just show a little respect for our elders, shall we, and go make me a cup of hot chocolate and a biccy, before I take off my belt to you and tan your hide big time.'

There was a short lull in the conversation then while I taught Clive some manners. I don't know if he enjoyed having his head trapped in the oven door all that much, but it seemed to quieten him down a bit and to help him regain a sense of perspective.

'Now look, Clive,' I said. 'I don't care what it says on any certificates or any mix-ups any midwives might have made. The fact is that I am still the eldest. The reason why is because you've got your measurements wrong. The eldest of twins isn't the one who's born first, it's the one who does the first wee-wee, and that was me. So you're still the youngest on a technicality.'

Clive looked a bit overawed when I told him that. This is Clive's trouble in a lot of ways – he is inclined to believe what people tell him. This is not a good policy, in my view, at least not when the information in question is coming from your brother. Some people you can trust, and some you can't, and brothers don't come into the first category.

He scratched his head.

'I didn't know that,' he said.

'Oh yes,' I told him. 'It's a well-known fact in the medical profession. Whenever there's twins and they're not sure who's the eldest, the decider is always who does the first wee-wee.'

'You sure?' he said.

'Positive,' I told him.

'You sure it's not the biggest wee-wee?'

'No,' I said. 'Size isn't what counts. It's being first that determines it.'

'What about poos?' he said.

'We don't talk about them,' I told him. 'We're too polite.'

Clive furrowed his eyebrows then, which is what he does when he's trying to do hard thinking. Clive cannot do hard thinking without the accompaniment of facial gestures. Mind you, even with the facial gestures, he still doesn't find it easy.

'Hang on,' he said. 'How do you know that you were the first to do a wee-wee and not me?'

'I can remember doing it,' I said. 'There I was, doing wee-wees, while you were still lying there staring at the ceiling in the maternity ward, thinking "Where am I?" and "What am I doing here?" and "What time do they come round with the pizza?"'

He did a bit more eyebrow furrowing.

'How can you remember what you did back when you were only five minutes old?' he said, sounding suspicious.

'I kept a diary,' I told him.

'Oh,' he said.

'In my mind,' I hastily added, to forestall further questioning. 'Not a written diary, obviously, as I hadn't yet learnt to write, back in those five-minute-old days. It was more or a sort of video diary – a kind of DVD diary – in my head.'

Clive did some heavy-duty, extra-strength with additional vitamins eyebrow furrowing.

'You mean you've got a DVD player?' he said. 'In your head? So where do the discs fit in? Do you slot them in through your gob?'

To be perfectly honest, I began to get a little tetchy at this point. It seems to me sometimes that Clive is not just being stupid, he is being wilfully stupid, like he is doing it to get on people's nerves.

'Now see here, Clive,' I said. 'It's my memory I'm talking about. My memory in my brain in my head. I'm not talking about having a DVD player stuck up my gob. But if you go on deliberately getting hold of the wrong ends of sticks, you won't just have a DVD player in your gob, you'll have the TV set and your entire CD collection in there as well. Got me? And as for where I'll stick your iPod, well, I'm not going into details.'

Clive went a bit quiet then, as he does sometimes

29

when he is thinking over what you have said and trying to work out if there are any big words in it above four letters long, which he might need to look up in a dictionary. (Not that he can spell 'dictionary'.)

'So you're the eldest then, are you?' he said.

'In wee-wee terms,' I said, 'yes.'

'I see,' Clive said.

'And wee-wee terms are what matter,' I said again, just to emphasize the point.

'Hmm,' Clive said.

'You can say that again,' I said.

'Hmm,' Clive said.

'I said you could,' I said. 'I didn't say you had to.'

'Hmm,' Clive said.

'If you say "Hmm" again, Clive . . .' I said, and I reached for the oven door . . .

'So what you're saying, if I get you right,' Clive said, 'is that you reckon you're the oldest after all.'

'Isn't that just what I've spent the past five minutes saying, Clive?' I said.

He furrowed not only his eyebrows but his ears as well.

'Dunno,' he said.

'Well, it is,' I told him. 'So I'm back to being the eldest. Any objections?'

For a moment it looked as though Clive was going to have many and several objections, but then he brightened up, and a smile lit his face, just as if it was a birthday candle.

'So that means I won't have to be the eldest any more, and be in charge, and have to be a leader of men, and say things like, "Look lively, now," and "Mind how you go," and "Best foot forwards," and stuff?'

'Those days, Clive,' I said, 'are behind you. What do you say?'

'Great,' he said. 'It's a deal!'

So Clive went back to being the youngest, and I went back to being the eldest. It was all accomplished as simply and as painlessly as that, and all over in a moment.

But the odd thing was that even as Clive went off whistling to himself, heading up to his room to give his stick insects a fresh coat of varnish and wood preservative, I couldn't help but feel that somehow I had been short-changed, and had come out the worst from the deal. It was strange that, because I'd got what I'd wanted – but now that I had it, I wasn't sure that I'd really wanted it at all in the first place. I sort of envied Clive his carefree existence as the youngest in the family, and I felt all burdened down with responsibilities again. I almost went after him and told him that I hadn't been first to do a wee-wee after all. But on reflection, I decided to leave it. Now that I was the eldest again, I'd be able to set an example to Clive and to give him spiritual guidance and to show him the right path to take for a good and honest life. And if he didn't listen, I'd be entitled to kick him up the backside.

So I decided to leave things as they were – at least for the time being.

Dad had said that he was going to ring Mrs Dominics and tell her that he couldn't accept her offer as soon as we got home, but once we were home, he kept putting it off, as though hoping that some miracle would happen and the Archangel Gabriel would appear and take me and Clive off his hands for six weeks.

'Dad . . .' I said, as I helped him get the tea ready. (Clive wasn't helping, he was sitting trying to read his book. Clive has had his book for several years now and is making good progress with it. Only a few more pages and he will be at the end of chapter one. Although he wasn't helping with the tea, it was his turn to do the washing up after – or 'breaking the plates' as washing up is known when Clive does it.) 'Dad,' I said, 'you still haven't told us what this offer of Mrs Dominics's is about.'

'Oh, it's nothing,' Dad said, in the way that people do when what they mean is just the opposite. 'Nothing important.'

'But what is it, Dad?' I said. 'What is this opportunity?'

Dad sighed and sat down at the table while the

sausages cooked under the grill.

'Well,' he said, 'it's like this. Now, you know Mrs Dominics is a very rich lady?'

'Yes, Dad,' I said. 'We've heard her diamonds clattering when she walks.'

'Well, amongst the many properties she has, as well as the restaurant here, she also owns the Hotel Royal—'

'The Hotel Royal?' Clive echoed. Clive had never heard of it, but then Clive has not heard of a lot of things. I don't think Clive has even heard of himself.

'It's a big hotel in London,' Dad said. 'In the West End. In fact it's a huge hotel, one of the best in the world. It's got five stars and it's used by the rich and famous, by film actors and rock singers and company directors and billionaires and all sorts.'

'Cor,' said Clive. 'Is it like that bed and breakfast we stayed at once, in Weston-super-Mare? The one where they kept the teaspoon on a piece of string?'

'A bit, Clive. But a lot bigger,' Dad said. 'And a lot more luxurious.'

'So what did Mrs Dominics want you to do there, Dad?' I asked.

'Well,' Dad said, and he looked a bit wistful, like it was a chance gone and an opportunity lost, something he'd always wanted to do but would never be able to now, 'she wants me to manage it.'

'Manage it! The whole hotel! Wow!'

'Well, she was very kind,' Dad explained, 'and said

she felt I'd done such a good job with the restaurant – and what with my experience on the cruise liners and everything – that she'd like me to stand in for the manager for six weeks, while he's away travelling the world and seeing how things are done in all the other grand hotels.'

'Cor, Dad,' Clive said. 'That would be great. To be the manager of a five star hotel, in the middle of London! Where all the rich and famous go! Cor, that would be fantastic. You could take sneaky photographs of them scratching themselves and sell them to the newspapers.'

'Yes,' Dad said. 'Yes, it would – though I don't think that's quite the idea.' Then he went to the grill to turn the sausages, and to check the chips in the oven. 'Still, never mind . . .' And he put on some peas as well.

I looked at Clive and Clive looked at me, and I guess we both thought the same. We're nothing but millstones, we thought, around Dad's neck. We weigh him down and hold him back and he can't do what he wants to because of us. I felt really bad then, that Clive should be holding Dad back like that, and that not even Grandma and Granddad would have him for six weeks as he was such an unruly handful and a king-sized pain in the trousers.

'We're sorry, Dad,' I said, 'that we're stopping you going and realizing your ambitions and stuff.'

Dad gave us a smile and tried to be cheerful.

'You're not doing any such thing,' he said. 'I'd

rather be here with you two than run any swanky hotel, and that's the truth.'

The way he said it, I felt it was the truth, but underneath the truth he couldn't help but feel a little bit regretful that things had turned out as they had.

'We can play at hotels, if you like, Dad,' Clive offered. 'You can stay in bed in the morning and we can be room service. We can cook you some eggs.'

'No, no, that's all right, thanks, Clive,' Dad said. 'I'd feel safer if you didn't.'

The microwave pinged then to say the peas were done, and as it did there was another ping, only this one came from the doorbell.

'Oh great,' Dad said. 'Perfect timing. Who's that at the door now, just when we're about to sit down to tea?'

'I'll get it,' I said. 'Won't you, Clive?'

So Clive, being the youngest, went and answered the door. We heard voices and when he came back he was followed by a lady – Mrs Dominics herself.

'John . . . boys . . .' she said, and she looked around the kitchen in an approving sort of way. A lot of ladies think that as we are three blokes on our own we live like pigs, but we don't. We're pretty tidy really, and although Clive has pig-like tendencies, such as his cereal bowl in the mornings, for example, which is so big it is practically a trough, we don't let him get out of hand.

'Well, what a surprise . . .' Dad said, eyeing the cooking food with dismay.

Mrs Dominics took it all in.

'Oh dear,' she said. 'I've called at the wrong time.'

'No, not at all,' Dad said, though it was plain that she had.

'I had Chaswick drive me over to visit a friend,' she said, 'and as I was passing, John, I thought I would drop in and see if you had made your mind up yet, regarding my little offer.'

Dad looked a bit glum.

'Ah, yes, Mrs Dominics,' he said. 'I was going to ring you after we'd eaten.'

'Well, now I'm here, you don't have to. You can tell me now, John,' she said. 'And I hope the news is going to be good news. Just tell me and I'll be off and let you get on with your dinner.'

'You don't mind if I dish it out?' Dad said. 'Or it'll burn.'

'Carry on.'

'Well, Mrs Dominics,' Dad said, 'I'm afraid that as much as I'd like to accept your offer – because it is a wonderful opportunity – I'll have to turn it down. You see, I'd hoped that the boys' grandparents would be able to take them for the summer, but unfortunately they feel that they're getting too old and, well, boys . . .'

'Will be boys,' Mrs Dominics nodded, and I was

interested to see that she had inside information on that subject.

'Look, Mrs Dominics . . .' Dad paused as he looked down at the sausages. 'I seem to have cooked too many of these,' he said. 'Would you care for a sausage?'

'Oh, lovely,' Mrs Dominics said. 'No need for a fork. Just a plate will do. I'll have it in my fingers. And would you have one to spare for Chaswick? He's outside in the car.'

'I'll take him one,' I offered.

So Dad put a sausage on a plate and I took it out for Chaswick.

The Rolls Royce was surrounded by some of the neighbourhood children, all with grubby hands. Chaswick was standing at the bonnet with his arms folded, looking at them threateningly. Touch that paintwork, his eyes seemed to say, and you're dead.

'Mr Chaswick,' I said. 'Mrs Dominics sent me out with a sausage for you.'

I think that if it hadn't come courtesy of Mrs Dominics, he might have stuck it up someone's nose – probably mine.

'Oh lovely,' he said. 'Too kind.'

He took the sausage and I went back into the house, but I suspect that while my back was turned he threw the sausage over the hedge, because I saw our cat later with bits of sausage in his whiskers, and I certainly hadn't given him a bite of mine.

As I returned to the kitchen, Clive and Dad were sitting at the table eating, while Mrs Dominics nibbled her sausage.

'But really, John,' she was saying. 'There's no reason why that should be a problem. If you can't find anyone to look after the boys while you're managing the hotel in London, then the solution is perfectly obvious . . .'

'You mean get in a baby-sitter?' Clive said. 'For six weeks?'

'That might be a problem, Mrs Dominics,' I said. 'Clive was blacklisted from the baby-sitting circle years ago, back when he was still a baby. It was due to something he did involving his nappy, when he took it off and waved it round his head and threw it straight into—'

'I don't think Mrs Dominics wants to hear about that actually,' Dad interrupted. But in my opinion he was wrong, because she looked pretty interested to me.

'No, no,' Mrs Dominics said. 'I wasn't thinking of baby-sitters or anything like that. No, John, all I was going to say was that if you cannot leave the boys behind, then why not take them with you?'

Nobody spoke for a few seconds. We just looked at each other. Me and Clive were thinking the same thinking. Six weeks, we were thinking, swanky hotel, we were thinking, five stars, we were thinking, middle of London, we were thinking, in the posh bit too, we were thinking, with waiters waiting on us hand and foot, and lots of snacks on the room service, twenty-four hours a day. Yes, we were thinking. Not a bad idea at all.

But Dad had gone a bit pale.

'Em, well, Mrs Dominics, that's a very generous offer.'

'Not at all, John,' she said. 'While you're working the staff can keep an eye on them. There's plenty there to keep them amused. There's a gym, a pool, a TV and a games room, there's London on your doorstep, so there's no reason why anyone should be bored . . .'

'B-but –' Dad was saying, 'it's just – I mean – the three of us – six weeks – in the one room.'

Mrs Dominics looked amazed.

'Oh no,' she said. 'It wouldn't be a room. Not as you would be acting manager. Not if you'd have the boys with you. No, naturally, one room would be nowhere near enough. I would give you a suite.'

Clive looked up from his sausages when he heard the word 'suite'.

'Sweets?' he said. 'Will there be sweets?'

'Not that sort of sweet, Clive,' I said. 'The other sort. The sort you live in!'

Clive didn't look very happy. It was all going wrong for him.

'So you mean,' he said, 'that instead of going to

London and living in a posh hotel, we have to go there and live in a sweet?'

'No, Clive—' Dad began. But it's hard to get a word in when Clive is on full throttle.

'How can we live in a sweet!' Clive was wailing. 'It'll never be big enough. And how are we going to get inside? And what if we do get inside, but someone comes and eats it while we're in there?'

'Clive—'

'No way,' Clive went on. 'No way am I going to go and live in a sweet. I'll get all sticky. And what happens when it rains? And just say it's a sherbet lemon and I end up getting eaten away by the acid – no way. I mean, I'm prepared to consider living inside some chocolate, like a big Easter egg or something like that, but I'm not getting inside any sweets.'

Mrs Dominics sat chewing her sausage and looking at Clive as though he were a very rare and unusual species of wildlife in a highly specialized zoo – the sort where they keep animals on the edge of extinction.

'No, Clive, dear,' she said. 'That sort of sweet is spelt s-w-e-e-t. The kind of suite I'm talking about is spelt s-u-i-t-e. It is a collection of rooms. Like an apartment. You have bedrooms, bathrooms, a balcony, a lounge – in fact the suites in the Hotel Royal are extremely opulent, ornate and highly commodious.'

'That's all well and good, Mrs Dominics,' Clive

said, 'and I appreciate your offer. And I'm sure opulent is all well and good, but personally, I prefer a bit of comfort.'

'Clive,' Dad said. 'Opulent means luxurious.'

'Oh,' Clive said. 'Oh. Yes. Well, of course I knew that. I was just making out I didn't, to prevent any embarrassing silences in the conversation.'

'Very kind of you, Clive,' Dad said.

'So, John?' Mrs Dominics said, finally coming to the end of her sausage and the end of her visit. 'I'd better not keep Chaswick waiting, he's due home soon. In fact he should have been off-duty an hour ago. But he still has to drive me back.'

'Well, Mrs Dominics . . .' Dad began, but he trailed off as he looked at the faces staring at him. There was me, trying to seem indifferent to it all, and not trying to put any pressure on Dad in any way, and then there was Clive.

You could tell what Clive was thinking from about two hundred miles away. The thoughts seemed to be all but bubbling out of him. London. Luxury. Big sweets. Pool. Room service. Big fluffy towels. Dressing gowns. Spoilt rotten. Free food. Twenty-four hours a day. A chocolate under your pillow every evening when the maid came to turn the bed down.

And then you could tell what Dad was thinking. He was thinking: Clive. On the loose. On the rampage. Luxury hotel. Expensive ornaments. Big mirrors. Broken glass. Never be able to pay for all the damage.

But another part of him was thinking: great opportunity. Once in a lifetime. Manager of the Hotel Royal.

'Well?' Mrs Dominics said. 'I don't like to hurry you, John, but what's it going to be?'

Dad looked from Clive to me and back again.

'Listen, you two,' he said. 'If I say yes to you coming with me, do you promise to be on your best behaviour – your very best behaviour—'

'Yes, Dad,' Clive said. But by then he'd have said 'Yes, Dad,' to anything, just as long as he got to go and live in a sweet.

'I haven't finished. Do you promise to be on your best behaviour for the whole of your summer holiday, for all the time you'll be in the hotel, for every day of those six weeks and every minute of each of those days. Well?'

I nodded with my best and sincerest nod.

'Promise, Dad,' I said.

'And you, Clive?'

'Promise,' Clive said. 'Cross my heart and hope to die. Cut my nose off and stick it in my ear.'

And I'm sure he meant it when he said it. I'm sure he honestly did. Because he's not a bad bloke at heart, is Clive. He's not one to deliberately break a promise or anything like that.

He just tends to forget he's made any.

About ten seconds after he's made them.

So there we were. There was no more time. Mrs Dominics had made her offer and now she had to go. It was yes, or it was no.

'Well, John?'

'We'd love to, Mrs Dominics. And thank you, for giving me – for giving us – such a wonderful opportunity.'

'Ah, John,' Mrs Dominics said, as she gathered her expensive coat around her, her necklaces and diamonds sparkling and rattling as she put it on. She was probably wearing about a million pounds, and that was just on her left hand. It was hard to say how old she was, probably about a hundred and two. But she had a nice old face, fringed with pure-white hair. 'John,' she said, 'it isn't a fraction of what you and your family have given to me.'

I didn't have a clue what she was on about. The only thing we'd ever given her that I knew about was the sausage.

'I'll be in touch about the arrangements,' she said. 'I'll get my secretary to ring you in the morning. And please,' she said, as we all trooped out to see her to the door, 'please don't worry about taking the boys with you. I'm sure there won't be any problems at all. In fact, they'll be an asset to the hotel. Now, if you'll excuse me, I'll be off. And remember. Don't worry. Nothing can go wrong.'

The times I've heard that – nothing can go wrong.

You never want to say a thing like that. Not when Clive's around. The number of times Clive has proved those theories to be groundless, and yet people go on believing them. 'Nothing can go wrong,' they say. Then Clive arrives.

Off Mrs Dominics went. Chaswick opened the door of the Rolls Royce for her and did his best to swat away the swarm of curious kids in Manchester United shirts, which had congregated around the car. Mrs Dominics told him to drive away slowly, in case he ran over their feet.

We went back into the house to have some yoghurts for pudding. 'I'll need to get myself a new dark suit,' Dad was saying. 'And a few more white shirts. You need to be well dressed when you're the manager of a hotel like the Royal.'

Clive sat at the table, spooning yoghurt into the bottomless pit of his cakehole.

'We're going to London,' he said. 'To live in a sweet.'

Dad looked at him, with slight apprehension and a mind full of second thoughts.

'I hope I've not made a mistake,' he said.

But if he had, he'd already made it, and it was too late to do much about it. He'd given his word now to Mrs Dominics, and if there's one thing Dad says you always have to do, it's that you have to keep your word.

4

London

Of course, the truth of the matter is that Clive and me were used to high-living and being pampered, as we had already had a spell of it on an all-star cruise liner.

Things like gold bath taps, and hot and cold running water, and knives and forks, and unlimited supplies of lemonade, and soap in little wrappers are nothing to me and Clive. We take that kind of thing in our stride, for we are used to luxuries like that, things such as caviare and chunky marmalade.

Admittedly when we were on our ocean cruise we had to travel for most of the journey as stowaways down in the bilges of the ship in what became known to us as rat class, but once we were up on deck, we lived like millionaires. So swanky hotels are nothing special as far as we are concerned.

'I was born for luxury,' Clive said to me as we

packed our cases to get ready to go to London and move into the Hotel Royal for the long weeks of the summer holiday. 'By rights,' he said, 'I should be living in Buckingham Palace with the Royal Family, or maybe round at Number Ten, Downing Street with the Prime Minister. I'm just slumming it here really,' he said, 'associating with the likes of you. As a matter of fact, I'm only here by mistake, see. In fact, I wouldn't be surprised if there had been a mix-up at the hospital and you're not actually my brother at all.'

'Oh, is that so, Clive?' I said. 'And so who do you think you are, exactly? And where do you rightly belong – apart from round at the local loony bin or the nearest pig farm?'

'The way I see it,' Clive said, as he sat on his suitcase in a fruitless effort to close the lid – he had far too much stuff in there. I'd already told him that his mountain bike would never go in unless he took the wheels off first. 'The way I see it is that I was born of noble and aristocratic parentage, but due to a clerical error, I ended up living with common people instead. But one day, the truth will out, and then I shall be able to claim my birthright.'

I wasn't too happy at hearing some of this and I asked Clive to clarify a few things.

'When you say "common people", Clive,' I said. 'Who do you have in mind exactly?'

Clive looked all around the room, as if

searching for something. Finally his gaze fell upon yours truly.

'Well – you,' he said.

'Me?' I said.

'Yes,' he said.

'I see,' I said. 'I see. So I'm common, am I?'

'Seems that way,' Clive nodded. 'It can't be helped, but there you go.'

Well, I wasn't able to let a thing like that go by without making some small comment and taking appropriate action, just to let Clive know that he was being a touch on the rude side. So that was what I did, and just after I'd finished putting Clive straight on the matter of who was common and who wasn't, Dad came up to see how our packing was going.

'Are you two nearly ready yet?' he said.

'Almost, Dad,' I told him, zipping up my stuff in my toilet bag.

'Where's Clive?' Dad asked. 'And what's that funny groaning sound? And why does Clive's suitcase seem to be moving about?'

'Clive's suitcase, Dad?' I said. 'How do you mean?'

But when I looked at it, I saw exactly what he meant, for it almost seemed to be alive, as if something inside were threshing around, and odd moaning noises were coming from it.

'Oh dear, Dad,' I said. 'It looks as if Clive has gone and accidentally packed himself away in his suitcase.

I wonder how that could have happened? He must have done it while my back was turned.'

'Clive!' Dad said, sounding a touch impatient. 'Will you please stop messing about and come out of there.'

'*Ug gug gug gug gug ug*,' Clive said.

'What's he saying?' Dad said.

'I think he's saying he can't open it from the inside,' I said.

Dad let him out.

'For heaven's sake, Clive,' he said. 'We're leaving in an hour. Will you please stop mucking around and zipping yourself up in your suitcase!'

'But it wasn't—'

'I've got no time to listen to your excuses right now, Clive,' Dad said. 'Just finish your packing. I expect you both to be finished and ready to go in the hour.'

And off he went. I suppose he was too busy to ask how Clive had managed to zip himself up in his suitcase without some outside assistance. In some ways, that was just as well.

'I'll get you for that,' Clive said. 'You'll be sorry you ever did that, you'll see.'

But Clive's threats have never bothered me much, as he is mostly all talk and no action. Anyway, he looked all right in the suitcase. It sort of suited him, in my opinion.

'You should wear a suitcase all the time, Clive,' I

said. 'It makes you seem better-looking. Yes, you could wear a suitcase during the week, and at the weekends you could go round in a sports bag.'

'Just don't walk down any dark alleys,' Clive muttered, trying to sound threatening. 'Or you'll end up in a duffle bag – chopped up in small pieces.'

'You and whose army?' I scoffed. For I knew that Clive did not have an army, and wasn't ever likely to either.

We got on with our packing then. I was careful not to turn my back on Clive when I went to close my suitcase. For Clive can be very petty-minded and vengeful at times, and all he ever thinks of is evening up scores and of getting his own back for imagined slights and injuries.

School had only finished for the summer the day before. Everyone had been asking everyone else where they were going for their holidays. Some had been going to Spain and some had been going to Cornwall, but we seemed to be the only ones who were going to London.

'Are you ready?' Dad called up from downstairs. We carried the suitcases and the bags down and loaded them into the car.

We have only a little car really. This is because although we are used to living the high life and staying in the best places, we don't actually have much money. Mrs Dominics pays Dad a good salary for running The Stowaway restaurant, but he says that we cost him a small fortune, that we are always outgrowing things and needing new trainers about once a fortnight, and the money soon vanishes. He says it's a shame there isn't a bigger age difference between us, then one could pass his old clothes and shoes on to the other.

I'm glad this isn't the case, though I haven't said so. If I'd been a few years younger than Clive and had had to wear his old clothes, it would have been horrible, especially if I'd had to have had his old pants. Clive's pants are actually what is known as 'unfit for human consumption' and are a hazard to passers-by and the general public. In fact if Clive's pants ever escaped from the house and went on the rampage, it is my opinion that the police would go after them with armed marksmen before Clive's pants did any damage and terrified little toddlers.

I think that the police would probably corner them somewhere and give them the choice of either giving themselves up or being shot. Clive's pants do not give up easily, however, and are extremely dangerous. Even our washing machine looks frightened of them. I'm sure it isn't, as it is just a machine. But it seems that way. It looks as if it is about to run off and hide in a corner whenever laundry baskets with Clive's pants in them are brought into the vicinity.

It was a bit of a squeeze getting all the cases into the car, and me and Clive had to sit with bags on our laps. It was my turn to sit in the front though, so Clive had most of the luggage with him. He kept kicking me in the back of the seat as we drove along, but when I told him to pack it in, he said that it wasn't him, it was the rucksack that was doing it. Dad told us both to stop arguing, which I thought was unfair, as I wasn't arguing at all, it was Clive.

It was about a three-hour car journey from where we lived to get to London. We'd always lived by the sea too, so it was quite a change for us to be going somewhere that was basically dry-land.

'There is a big river in London though,' Dad said, as we drove up the motorway. 'The Thames is deep and wide enough to take some big ships too. I think they've even had the odd submarine navigate its way up the river. Oh, and we must go up in the London Eye while we're there. That's next to the Thames.'

'What's the London Eye?' I asked.

'It's like a great big wheel,' Dad explained. 'A big Ferris wheel, like you see at fairgrounds, only much, much bigger, and it revolves very slowly, and you can go up in it and get the most fantastic views of the whole of London.'

'Is there a London Nose as well as a London Eye, Dad?' Clive asked. 'Can we go up in the London Nose too? Can we go up one nostril and come back down the other one?'

'No, Clive,' Dad said in his 'don't be stupid' tone of voice. 'There isn't a London Nose.'

'How about the London Ear then, Dad? Can we visit that? Is there wax in it? Can you stick your finger inside?'

'There isn't a London Ear, Clive, just the London Eye.'

'How about the London Toenail, Dad—?'

'Clive. That'll do!'

But that was always Clive's trouble, he didn't know where to stop.

'How about the London Armpits, Dad?'

'That's *enough*, Clive.'

'The London Bum?'

'Clive, I'm warning you . . .'

Clive shut up about the London Bum then and we drove on in silence for an hour. Once we were near enough to our destination for it not to be worth turning back again though, he started up once more.

'Dad, when we get to London, when we've visited the London Eye, can we visit the London Guts as well?'

'There's no such thing as the London Guts, Clive.'

'The London Kidneys then, Dad?'

'Clive—'

'Can we visit the Great Wart of London then, Dad?'

By then I'd had enough too.

'Don't be stupid, Clive,' I said. 'Stop showing yourself up. And don't show your ignorance. Everyone knows that the Great Wart isn't in London.

The Great Wart is in China. Isn't it, Dad? That's where it is, isn't it? You're just so ignorant you are, Clive, and you never pay any attention in class. If you did you'd know all about the Great Wart of China. So pipe down and stop showing yourself up.'

We drove on into London. Dad seemed to find something funny. I don't know what, as I couldn't see anything funny, but he seemed to find something vastly amusing.

'Great Wart of China,' he kept muttering. I don't know why. It was as if he'd never heard of it, and yet I'd always thought of him as quite good on the old general knowledge.

As we left the motorway and drove deeper into London, the buildings around us seemed to grow taller and taller and move closer and closer together. We passed some grubby-looking rows of terraced houses, and then some elegant squares of what Dad said were Regency buildings. There were cars everywhere, three or four lanes deep; there were mad cyclists too, weaving in and out of the traffic, some of them were couriers, carrying bags full of letters and parcels to deliver. Apparently you could get across inner London on a bicycle faster than in a car.

'Cor – look!' Clive said, his nose pressed up against the window. He didn't say what to look at, just to look, and he was right in a way, because there was so much to see it was hard to single any one thing out as deserving more attention than another.

There was everything in London. Shops and cafés and cars and taxis and people of all shapes and sizes and colours and religions from all the countries in the world. Some of them were still in their national costumes; there were saris and burkas and veils and white robes, there were men in baggy trousers and some in vivid African shirts. There were Indian people and a group of blond-haired, fair-skinned people who might have come from Scandinavia, and some Japanese people, and some Italian-looking people. But more than anything it was just people – the sheer quantity and number of them. People everywhere. People busy, people in a hurry, people beeping their car horns, people hurrying from buses or disappearing down into holes in the ground where the tube trains ran. It was just people, people, people, and cars, cars, cars.

'Wow,' said Clive. 'What would you do if you got lost? You'd never get found again.'

'Don't get lost,' Dad said. 'If you do, find a policeman and tell him you're living at the Hotel Royal, remember.'

'Yes, Dad,' Clive said. 'Not that I'm planning on getting lost.'

But then Clive never plans on most things he ends up doing.

5

The Hotel

'Oi!' a voice yelled. 'You can't park there!'

We had just pulled into a parking space behind an automated barrier at the rear of the Hotel Royal. There were only about two dozen parking spaces there in total. The one we had stopped in had the words *Hotel Manager* printed on a little plate by the fence.

'We're lucky to get our own parking space,' Dad had said, just before the voice had started shouting. 'Parking spaces in central London are like gold dust.'

Clive peered out of the window.

'Doesn't look much like gold dust to me,' he said. 'Looks more like a car park.'

'No need to take things so literally, Clive,' Dad said.

'Oi! Clear off! It's you I'm talking to! You there

in the bubble car! You lot, in the dinky-mobile!'

Dad looked up to see a red-faced man in what had to be a porter's uniform standing next to our car and looking down at us with a very angry expression. He looked a bit like an irate cauliflower – only red. His uniform was decorated with gold braid and he had two stripes on his arm.

Dad wound the window down a bit.

'I beg your pardon?' he said. 'Are you talking to us?'

'Yeah, you. That's right. You and the two monkeys in the back. You can't park here. This is a reserved space. This is for the manager. So hop it, before I call security and have you towed away.'

Well, in the circumstances, it would have been only too easy for Dad to have lost his temper with the porter, or for him to have stood on his dignity and got a bit hoity-toity with him – especially as Clive was sitting there trying to egg Dad on, saying things like, 'Go on, hit him, Dad. He's just a big nobody. Lay one on him, Dad, and show him who's who.'

Fortunately our Dad is not like that, as he much prefers the soft answer and the diplomatic approach in order to defuse potentially explosive situations.

'Be quiet, Clive,' he hissed.

But 'Go on, Dad,' Clive insisted. 'Edge the car forwards and park it on his foot.'

Dad further rolled down the window of our

'dinky-mobile' as the porter had called it. I saw that the porter was wearing a name badge with the word *Lester* on it.

'What's the matter?' Lester said. 'Didn't you hear me? Have I got to spell it out for you? Clear off. This is a posh hotel here and we don't let the riff-raff in. This parking space is reserved for Mr Johnson, the new acting manager. You can't just stop and leave your car here while you go off for a cheeseburger. Hop it. You and the monkey boys are making the place untidy.'

Personally, I took exception to being referred to as a monkey boy, though when I looked at Clive, I could see that Lester had a point. Clive definitely has something of the missing-link about him, and I have noticed that whenever we visit the zoo, the gorillas get very excited at the sight of Clive, and the chimpanzees bang on the glass and make 'come on in – the water's lovely' gestures at Clive, sort of beckoning him over to join them, as if they recognize him as one of their own and a kindred spirit, and want him to sit with them in the big rubber tyre.

'As a matter of fact, Lester,' Dad said, as politely and as sweetly as he could, 'and I hate to say this, but I am Mr Johnson.'

Well, if Lester had been red before, he was crimson now.

'W-w-wha . . . th-that . . . good heav . . . flipping . . . oh no.'

'Afraid so,' Dad said.

'You're Mr Johnson?'

'I am indeed.'

'And the monkey boys – that is, the two young men . . . ?'

'My sons. I believe Mrs Dominics has arranged a suite of rooms for us?'

'Indeed she has, Mr Johnson, sir,' Lester said. 'And I do – I do apologize for the little misunderstanding.'

'That's all right, Lester,' Dad said. 'I'm sure you meant well.'

'I was just trying to keep your parking space for you, sir,' Lester said.

'Yes, very kind of you,' Dad said, clambering out of the car and having a stretch. 'But I think that perhaps you need to work on the social skills there a little, Lester.'

'Yes, sir, Mr Johnson,' Lester said. 'Can I help you with your bags?'

'OK-yah,' Clive drawled. 'Here you are, my man,' he said. 'You can start on my rucksack.'

'I wasn't talking to you, Monkey Boy,' Lester said out of the corner of his mouth in a low whisper, then he turned his attention back to Dad. 'Allow me, sir,' he said. 'Let me show you the way.'

'Thanks, Lester,' Dad said, passing him a couple of suitcases while Clive and I got out of the car.

'I just didn't think you'd be the new manager,' Lester said. 'I expected him to have, well . . .' Then he trailed off.

'A bigger car,' Dad said, finishing the sentence for him. 'Less of a dinky-mobile?'

'Sorry about that,' Lester said. 'Allow me.'

He took the rest of the cases and bags and loaded them all on to a trolley which was standing by the rear entrance to the hotel.

'The staff are all looking forward to meeting you,' Lester said. 'Mrs Dominics left instructions as to your accommodation, and the assistant manager, Miss Ellshire, is to give you a tour of the hotel.'

'Good,' Dad said. 'I'll look forward to meeting everyone and getting to know them.'

'This way then, sir,' Lester said. 'Follow me.'

He turned to push the luggage trolley, only to find that Clive was sitting on it. Lester was clearly torn between his duty as an employee not to offend the new manager and his basic instincts to get hold of Clive by the scruff of the neck and drop him, headfirst, into the nearest wheelie bin.

He didn't need to do either.

'Clive,' Dad said. 'Get off. And wait there a moment, I want a word with you.' He turned back to Lester. 'We'll catch you up in a second,' he said.

'Very good, sir,' Lester said, and went off with the trolley.

Dad squatted down so that he was level with us both.

'Now listen, you two,' he said, 'just because I'm the temporary manager here doesn't mean that either of you can take liberties with or be rude to the staff. Got it?'

'Yes, Dad,' I said.

'Yes, Dad,' Clive mumbled, though you could tell that he didn't really understand. In Clive's book if you've got it, you should make the most of it – you should flaunt it until it falls off.

'And if I get to hear that either of you has been taking liberties, there will be trouble with a capital T. OK? Now let's go in.'

But then trouble with a capital T is the only sort of trouble Clive knows. Clive is quite unfamiliar with trouble with a small t. To Clive, trouble with a small t wouldn't really be trouble at all.

Well, let me tell you. We thought that we'd seen luxury and five star comfort before, back when we stowed away on the cruise liner, but the decor and facilities of the Hotel Royal knocked spots off even that.

The whole hotel, from the word go, was all flock wallpaper and polished mahogany and deep, hushed carpets. Its corridors went on for miles and miles and there seemed to be more staircases than ways up Everest. There were lifts and dumbwaiters and several restaurants and conference rooms, along with lounges and bars and meeting places and a gymnasium and a huge swimming pool, along with a sauna, a steam room, a jacuzzi and a thermal spa. On top of all that there was a billiards room with a full-size snooker table in it, and there was a casino and gift shop and even a small, quiet chapel, where you could pop in for a moment if you felt like saying a prayer.

And that was only the bit of the hotel the customers saw. But behind the scenes it was every bit as grand, even when you didn't expect it to be. The kitchens were huge, with massive cooking ranges and enormous, walk-in fridges with stainless-steel doors. There were dozens of cooks and chefs and people chopping up vegetables and preparing salads and making bread and pastries and cakes. And then there were all the waiters and the porters and the maids, and then there was the laundry room, and there was the housekeeping room, and there were storerooms with stacks of linen and tablecloths and dressing gowns for the guests and – well, it just went on and on.

Everything about the Hotel Royal was on the grand and impressive scale, even the customers. They all seemed expensively dressed and dripping with money – accustomed to being waited on and having things their own way, and getting them done immediately too.

'Along here, Mr Johnson, sir,' Lester said. 'We'll

61

go up in the lift. This one is just for the penthouse. There are several other lifts for the guests and one for the staff.'

He wheeled our luggage into a smallish lift and we got in after it. It was a tight squeeze, but we all fitted in.

'The staff have their own lift then?'

'Own lift, sir, own dining room, own separate quarters – at least those who live in. And this is your floor, sir, coming up.'

We were at the top. It was a big hotel too, as I said, with a lot of floors. The lift stopped and the door pinged open.

'Here we are, sir. This is it.'

Only it wasn't. There was nothing there. At least there didn't seem to be at first. There was just another door. I'd expected the lift door to open on to a corridor, but no. We were faced by a big blank nothing.

'Your keys, sir,' Lester said.

He produced three plastic card-keys and inserted one of them into a lock in the door facing us. A small green light flashed in the lock. He took out the card and turned the door handle, and the door opened out into . . .

Well, it was absolutely massive. It was bigger than our house. We stood and gawped at it, all three of us.

'Th-this is it, is it?' Dad said.

'This is it, sir,' Lester confirmed. 'The manager's penthouse suite.'

Clive spoke for us all.

'Stone the crows!' he said. 'Flipping heck.'

'Allow me,' Lester said, and he hoisted in our luggage.

I nudged Clive with my elbow.

'A suite,' I said, 'with its own lift!'

'I've never lived in a place with its own lift, right in the living room,' Clive said. 'Ever.'

Lester overheard us.

'There is also the emergency staircase, should the lift not be working, sir,' he said. 'Over there.' And he indicated a door, discreetly situated in a corner, which led out to the fire stairs.

Four other doors led off from the sitting room. Two of them went to bedrooms, one of them opened out to a balcony, and the other opened up to reveal a huge drinks cupboard.

'For your relaxation,' Lester said.

There was so much drink in there you could have got relaxed permanently.

'The master bedroom is to the left, sir. The twin-bedded room to the right.'

'Can we go and see our room, Dad?'

'I suppose you'd better,' he said. 'But no quibbling about who's having which b—'

He was already too late.

'I want the bed by the window,' Clive said.

'Buzz off, Clive,' I told him, 'I saw it first!'

Lester leant over to Dad and spoke in a low and confidential tone.

'Would you like me to knock their heads together for you, sir?' he asked. 'It would be no trouble.'

'It's OK, thanks, Lester,' Dad said, 'but that won't be necessary. We'll find a compromise.'

'Very well, sir. I'll leave you to settle in.'

'Thanks,' Dad said. 'Give me twenty minutes, would you? Please tell the assistant manager that I'll meet her down at the desk. I'm going to need a crash course on what's going on here and a guided tour around the place.'

'I'll inform Miss Ellshire to expect you, sir.'

'Thanks. And what time do the staff eat? I was thinking of the boys.'

Lester went a funny colour again.

'They'll be eating?' he said. 'With the *staff*?'

'Well, I didn't think the main restaurant would be appropriate exactly.'

'No, sir. Of course not. Or we could send something up?'

'Oh yes, that might be nice. At least for tonight. Thank you.'

'The room service menu is over there, sir.'

Clive had already found it.

'What's a scallop?' he said. 'What's gourmet cuisine?' he wanted to know. 'What's cutlery?'

'We'll go through it in a minute,' Dad said. 'Thank you, Lester. I'll be down shortly.'

'Very well, sir,' Lester said, and he got back into the lift, closed the door, and slid back down to the ground floor.

6

The Penthouse Suite

We tried not to look too happy.

'Well, this isn't bad, is it?' Dad said.

'It's all right, I suppose,' Clive said.

'I'll have to try and get used to it, I guess,' I nodded.

'Of course,' Clive said, 'I'm not really used to roughing it, personally. I'm more used to luxury cruise liners and stuff, myself, but I dare say I could lower my sights and get used to the penthouse suite in a five star hotel. I mean, it's not as if it's for ever, and you can stand anything for a while.'

Then we went on the rampage, looking in every room and cupboard.

'Towels, Clive!' I said. 'Thick enough to live in!'

'A big telly,' he said. 'Size of a cinema screen! With cable and satellite and in-house movies.'

'Fridge!' I said. 'Full of drinks, snacks, assorted peanuts and chocolate bars!'

'Enormous toasted sandwich and waffle maker!' Clive yelled.

'No, Clive,' Dad said, 'that is not an enormous toasted sandwich and waffle maker. That is actually a trouser press.'

Clive stared at it, wincing and looking worried.

'Well, I'm not pressing my trousers in that,' he said. 'It looks like torture.'

'No, Clive,' Dad said. 'You take your trousers off first. You don't get into the trouser press with your trousers on. It's for trousers only.'

'Oh, right. Get it,' Clive said, and he went off to do a bit more rampaging around the suite. He found the free notepaper.

'Free notepaper!' he yelled.

'And envelopes!' I said.

'And a free biro with "Hotel Royal" on it! And a pencil called HB! That's a good name for a pencil, isn't it? I mean, it's better than Fido. I mean, Fido the pencil doesn't sound very good. But HB the pencil, it's bang on, isn't it?'

'Fantastic!' I said.

'Cor,' Clive said, 'the stuff you get, eh? Let's go and have a look at the balcony.' He opened the door to it. 'Balcony!' he yelled.

'Careful, Clive,' Dad said. But he needn't have worried. The balcony had a high rail around it to prevent drunks and idiots (like Clive) from accidentally falling off and down to the alleyway below. It was quite a large balcony too, with a small cast-iron table and chairs on it, so that you could go out and have your breakfast in the sunshine if you wanted to, in fine weather.

'Let's get drinks from the fridge,' Clive said, 'and take them outside.'

So that was what we did, while Dad hung some things up in the wardrobe and then had a quick shower before changing into his new suit for his meeting with the assistant manager, Miss Ellshire.

Clive and me got a drink from the fridge each, and a packet of jungle-fresh peanuts, and we sat at the balcony table, overlooking the city, and we ran an eye over the room service menu, trying to decide what to have for tea.

'I think I'll have fresh oysters, a bread roll, lemon cheesecake and chips,' Clive said. 'To begin with. Then for a main course, I'll have a packet of digestive biscuits and a lobster . . . let me see now . . . yes, and for pudding I'll have the ice-cream, and then for the cheese course – I'll have some cheese.'

'That's a good idea, Clive,' I said. 'Having cheese for your cheese.'

'Yes,' Clive said. 'I think I could be setting a trend in fashionable eating habits here. Cor, look,' he said. 'What's that?'

I looked down. For a moment I wondered what it

was too. It was a strange sight from where we were sitting. The penthouse was about fourteen storeys up from the ground, and while the Hotel Royal wasn't the highest building in the vicinity, it was high enough to afford quite a view of the London skyline. We could see the top of Nelson's statue in Trafalgar Square, and the flickering lights of Piccadilly illuminating the evening as the day turned to dusk. The whole city seemed like a picture of perfection and promise.

But in the alleyway down beneath us, way down on the ground directly under our balcony, all those floors below, it was a different story.

'It's cardboard, Clive,' I said. And sure enough, it was. There was a little village of cardboard houses down in the alleyway under the luxurious Hotel Royal and, as we watched, we could see people coming and going, arriving and departing.

'Dad,' I called. 'Come and see. What are those people doing in those cardboard boxes down there?'

Dad came out onto the balcony, freshly showered, his suit on, doing up his tie.

'They're living there, I'm afraid,' he said.

'Living?' I said. 'In cardboard boxes?'

'I'm afraid so. They're homeless, I guess, must be, or why else would they do it.'

'But why don't they go and live somewhere else?'

'Because they've nowhere else to go. Anyway, I must get ready.'

Dad went back inside. Clive and me stayed on the balcony a while, looking down at the little cardboard city in the alleyway by the hotel. It seemed weird somehow for us to be there in the penthouse suite, with room service on tap at the ring of a bell, with all the luxuries and conveniences, while down below us – just a short distance away – people were living in cardboard boxes, with no room service at all.

'It makes you count your blessings, really, doesn't it, Clive?' I said. 'Us up here, them down there. I know where I'd rather be.'

But Clive had his head stuck in the room service menu again.

'I've changed my mind about the lobster and digestive biscuits,' he said. 'I think I'll have a vegetarian pork chop and a fried Mars Bar in batter instead.'

Before Clive could get to the phone though and order up the sort of dinner for himself that would have put most people in hospital, Dad came out to say that he had already ordered for us.

'Something nice and simple, but sensible and tasty,' he said. 'I've ordered you both Dover sole and potatoes – with vegetables – with ice-cream for pudding.'

'Vegetables, Dad!' Clive said, growing increasingly distressed. 'But is that wise? For us to be eating vegetables, at this time of day?'

'Yes, it is,' Dad said. 'And see you *do* eat them.

No chucking them off the balcony – those poor people down there won't like it.'

'Don't worry, Dad,' I said. 'I'll see to it that Clive eats his vegetables. And that he chews them properly as well.'

'OK,' Dad said. 'I'm going down now to meet the assistant manager and all the staff and to get a feeling for the place. I'll be back in an hour or two. Will you be all right?'

'We'll be fine, Dad. Can we go exploring when we've had our tea?'

'Of course,' Dad said. 'But no running down the corridors and no annoying the guests. You hear me?'

'Yes, Dad,' we said.

'I mean it. If I hear that you've been annoying the guests in any way, then you'll have to spend the next six weeks cooped up in here. OK?'

'Can we use the swimming pool, Dad?' I asked.

'Yes,' he said. 'That'll be all right. It's always supervised, I understand. But while you're there, remember that whatever else you do, you must—'

'Behave ourselves and not annoy any of the guests.'

'That's it. OK. I'm going down to meet the staff. Your food should be up in twenty minutes or so. I'll see you both later.'

'OK, Dad.'

'OK, Dad.'

'And no fighting!'

He went to the door, opened it, and there was the lift in front of him. He got in, turned, waved to us, pressed the button, and disappeared.

'Cor, smooth, eh, Clive?' I said. 'Your own lift, coming right into your apartment.'

'Groovy,' Clive said. I saw he had the room service menu in his hand again. 'I think I might just ring up room service,' he said, 'and order a few extras to go with what Dad ordered.'

'Like what?' I said.

'Like some maple syrup, butterscotch sauce and pancakes.'

'Pancakes!' I said. 'You mean you're going to have Dover sole, potatoes and vegetables, along with maple syrup and pancakes?'

'Yeah,' Clive said. 'What about it?'

'That's disgusting,' I said. 'Absolutely revolting and full-scale pigging-out – order some for me as well.'

So that was what we had for dinner.

And very nice it was too . . .

The food was brought up on a trolley, on plates covered with big silver domes to keep it all warm. It was brought up by one of the room service waiters whose name – so his badge said – was Antonio. He had a strong foreign accent and a bald head, but he seemed very pleasant. He even served out the food for us on the dining table in the lounge of our suite.

But he didn't go away.

'Everythinga to youra liking, boys?' Antonio asked.

'A fine,' I said.

'A deada gooda,' Clive agreed.

Antonio gave us a smile, but he made no effort to move.

'What's he hovering for?' Clive said in a harsh whisper.

'I don't know,' I whispered back. 'Maybe he wants a tip?'

'But we're related to the manager,' Clive said. 'He can't expect a tip from us, can he?'

'Well, he's not going away,' I said, 'is he?'

He wasn't either. He was just sort of hovering and nodding his head and smiling.

'Give him your pocket money, Clive,' I said. 'He might go away then.'

'Get lost,' Clive said. 'Why don't you give him your pocket money?'

'I've spent it,' I said. I hadn't, but I knew that Clive hadn't spent any of his either, and he was just being tight-fisted.

'We'll have to give him something else then,' Clive said, 'if we haven't got any money. Let's give him the pencil.'

So Clive went and got the HB pencil and he gave it to Antonio.

'Thank you very much,' he said. 'That's for you.'

Antonio gave the pencil a sort of foreign-looking

look. He didn't seem actually all that pleased to get it. He put it into his top pocket, but he didn't go away.

'Now what?' Clive said.

'Give him one of the free envelopes,' I said. 'And one of those little cakes of soap from the bathroom, in the nice wrappers.'

But he still didn't go away.

Then I had an idea. I went to the fridge, opened it, and took two little miniature bottles of whisky out.

'Thanks, Antonio,' I said. 'For bringing our dinner up. And that's for you.'

His face lit up when I gave him the two little bottles of whisky.

'Ahm, thanka you, thanka you,' he said. 'You'rea good boys.'

Well, he was half right. One of us was.

'I come back for the plates later.'

Then he was off back down in the lift.

'Dead cool, isn't it,' Clive said, 'having your own lift?'

And I had to agree that it was.

After dinner, as Dad still hadn't come back yet, Clive and me decided to go exploring. We agreed that we would both be on our best behaviour and set a good example; after all, we were the manager's family and anything we did would reflect on Dad and we didn't want to let the side down.

'So no blowing your nose on your pullover, Clive, all right,' I said. 'And more importantly, no blowing your nose on other people's pullovers.'

'As if I would.'

'OK, come on then.'

We took our key-cards with us so we could get back into the room, then we went and summoned the lift. Up it came in seconds. We got inside.

'I wanna press the button,' Clive said. So I let him. Of course, being Clive, he pressed the wrong one and we ended up in the basement with the laundry.

'Nice one, Clive,' I said. 'Where to now? Shall we go potholing?'

'No need to be sarky,' he said, and he pressed another button. But instead of going up, we went down even further, to another level, a kind of sub-basement, called the cellar.

The lift door opened and a musty smell came in.

'Great, Clive,' I said. 'Now where have you brought us? So who lives down here then? Fungus the Bogeyman, I suppose, and the Phantom of the Opera, and a few coal miners.'

'Let's have a look and find out,' Clive said. 'I like places like this.' And he got out of the lift. I couldn't let him wander off on his own, so I had to get out too, to keep an eye on him.

The cellar was dimly lit. It was a kind of warren of passages and alcoves, and stacked up in the alcoves were dusty wine bottles in wooden racks.

They were probably all vintage wines, kept down there in the cool cellar until someone in the restaurant ordered one.

'Smells a bit here,' Clive said.

'You've brought us down to rat class again, haven't you, Clive?' I said. 'There's me, aspiring to better things all the time, like penthouse apartments and such, but all you can do is drag us back down to rat class at the first opportunity.'

'Rat class is interesting,' Clive said. 'You could hide down here and nobody would know.'

'You could die down here and nobody would know,' I said. 'Come on. Let's go back to the lift.'

It took us a while to find it again, but we did eventually, and we went up to the ground floor, to the lobby level, where the registration desk was for people arriving and departing.

The place was teeming. We took a look out of the front door. The street was full of cars and the pavements were packed with people. A doorman in a top hat stood at the hotel entrance, ready to whistle up cabs for the hotel guests and to give help and directions.

'All right, lads?' he said, as we emerged from the revolving door.

'Fine thank you.'

'Staying here with your parents, are you?'

'We're with the new manager – Mr Johnson. We're friends of Mrs Dominics.'

'Ah, right. Well then, so where are you off to now?'

'Oh, just looking.'

The street seemed so busy and congested and somehow intimidating that we decided to go back inside. There were expensive cars drawing up outside the Hotel Royal all the time, some of them driven by chauffeurs, and rich-looking, well-dressed people got out. There were even a few photographers loitering by the door, with cameras with flash-guns on them at the ready.

'They must be waiting in case any celebrities turn up,' Clive said. 'They're known as the snapperazzi.'

'Paparazzi!' I corrected him. But Clive is immune to being corrected.

'Yeah, the snapperazzi, like I said.'

The lobby was almost as busy as the street. A notice board announced that there was an awards ceremony of some kind taking place in the Ballroom. Men in evening suits and women in expensive-looking cocktail dresses were arriving and heading up the stairs.

'Come on,' Clive said. 'Let's go up and have a look. We might get an award for something.'

'Clive,' I said, 'if you read the notice board, you'll see that it's the National Hair Stylists' Banquet, Ball, and Annual Awards. I don't think it's the National Idiots' Awards. If it were, you might, I agree, stand a very good chance of winning something – probably the gold cup. Or if the hair stylists were handing out a special category award for Hair That Has Not Had A Comb Through It For At Least Five Years, you might get something too. As it is, they're just going to tell us to push off. So let's go exploring somewhere else.'

'No need to be sarky,' Clive said again; only with Clive there is often every need. Sarcasm is the only language he understands.

We spent a good hour or more wandering around the Hotel Royal on that first evening, and even then we didn't see it all. There were acres of corridors and hundreds of rooms. The dining rooms and the restaurants were crowded; there were people arriving, people departing; the bars were busy; the gift shop was crowded with foreign visitors buying souvenirs to take home.

We felt a bit lost, really, in the vastness of it all. There were hardly any other children that we saw, and the few we did see all looked posh and dripping with money. They passed us in the corridor giving us looks as if we were aliens.

Clive wanted to thump them, but I said that you could hardly go round thumping people just because they happened to be rich. But Clive said why not? I said it was because you couldn't help being born rich any more than you could help being born poor. Clive said maybe so, but a good thump would stop you from being stuck up and thinking you were better than people and that he was going to thump the next rich kid he saw, just to teach him some manners.

Unfortunately for Clive, the next rich kid we saw was twice Clive's size and looked like he spent his spare time weightlifting.

'So why didn't you thump him for being rich then, Clive?' I asked Clive when he had passed.

'Decided not to bother,' he said. 'He wasn't worth it. Let's go and have a look at the swimming pool.'

We headed off in the direction of the health club.

'I'll tell you one thing,' Clive said. 'At least there's no chance of us running into anyone from our school here. Just wait till we go back to school after the holiday and tell them all about us living in a swanky hotel with room service and our own lift.'

But Clive had spoken too soon, as we discovered when we turned the next corner. For who should we see walking towards us, carrying swimming towels and wearing flip-flops and hotel dressing gowns, with wet hair and steamed-up glasses.

It was none other than Mr and Mrs Swanker Watson, and their son, Swanker. Yes, it was Swanker himself – in person. It was Swanker Watson from our class.

7

Pure Swank

It might be worth saying a quick word on the subject of Swanker Watson here, if only to explain how someone with so much money ended up in the same class at the same school as me and Clive.

Although Swanker Watson's mum and dad are up to their eyeballs in dosh, they are of the opinion that they do not want Swanker to go to posh school, where he will only meet like-minded swankers of a similar disposition. They believe that this will be a handicap in later life for Swanker Watson and that in order for him to learn proper life skills and street-smarts, he should go to ordinary school where he will meet a wide variety of people, such as Clive.

People such as Clive do not exist in posh school, as they do not let them in. They have a sort of filtering system to keep the Clives out. They probably even have alarms and early-warning mechanisms, and if they ever spot any Clives trying to get in through the gates, they set the Rottweilers on them.

For all his money, Swanker Watson is not such a bad sort, and if he ever gets above himself, we remind him of his humble beginnings, for he once let slip that his granddad was a rat-catcher and rodent exterminator who used to go around with ferrets in his trousers and rubber bands round his ankles to stop them getting out. He also used to carry a large rubber hammer with him, in case he saw any cockroaches.

From these unpromising beginnings, Swanker's granddad set up a national pest-exterminating company called Ratatatat. The business was passed on to Swanker's dad when his grandfather died and is now worth millions and millions, which only goes to show that there is a lot of money in killing pests and getting rid of cat fleas.

There are fortunes to be made in this line of work and Clive once told me that when he grows up (or maybe *if* he grows up might be more accurate) he is going to set up his own private worm-exterminating company. When he told me that I said that I thought it was a good idea, for even if he never made any money, at least he would never go hungry. But I don't think he understood what I was on about.

Anyway, getting back to the Swanker Watsons, they send Swanker to ordinary school, like I said, where he rubs shoulders with ordinary people like me as well as people with learning deficiencies and behavioural difficulties like Clive. But once school is over, it is back to the big mansion for Swanker. No three-ups, two-downs for him. No, home is a big pad in the country, with more rooms than people to sleep in them.

The Swanker Watsons also like to spend their holidays in smart hotels and luxurious places, where there is no chance that they will run into any loutish behaviour and riff-raff and people with poor table manners who do not know their lobster skewers from their toothpicks.

Mrs Swanker Watson is quite highly-strung and given to attacks of the vapours. Mr Swanker Watson is not, but he is fond of a glass of whisky. He quite often goes on the wagon and doesn't touch a drop of alcohol for months. But then suddenly the wagon lurches on a corner, and he falls off.

I believe that Mr Swanker Watson's drinking binges can also be set off by stress and stressful situations.

It might be worth noting in this context that Clive is generally considered to be a form of stress by most people and that he should be avoided by those with weak hearts and hair-trigger bladders, as otherwise he can cause stampedes to the toilet.

'Well, look who it is!' Clive said, when we turned the corner and discovered Swanker Watson standing there looking a bit pudgy in his hotel dressing gown, with his towel under his arm and his swimming goggles still on. 'How are you doing, Swank? You look like Batman in those goggles.'

I noticed that Mr and Mrs Swanker had both gone pale. Mrs Swanker was clutching at the wall for support and Mr Swanker had the look about him of a man who has misplaced his bottle opener.

'Hiya, Clive!' Swanker said. 'What a surprise. What are you two doing here?'

It was a little difficult to make out at first just what Swanker was saying, for as well as still having his goggles on, he was also talking through his snorkel. He took it out and repeated what he had said in a more comprehensible manner.

'We live here, Swanker,' Clive said. 'We're permanent residents!'

'Permanent residents . . .' I heard Mrs Swanker Watson say in a tremulous voice, then she started looking in her handbag for something. 'Charles,' she said to Mr Swanker, 'have you seen my Valium?'

'Never mind that,' I heard Mr Swanker say, 'have you seen a wine waiter?'

'Permanent?' Swanker said. 'How do you mean? I thought you usually spend your holidays at your gran's – when you aren't stowing away on luxury cruise ships.'

'Nah,' Clive said. 'Not this year. We decided to

give Gran's a rest. They're getting a bit old to be honest and can't cope with boyish high spirits like they used to. And besides, Granddad's booked into the garage to get his corduroy trousers serviced, as the tread's getting thin on them and they're probably nearly illegal, and he also needs to get some new long-johns fitted – or something like that – so it wouldn't be convenient. So we've come up to London. With our dad. He's managing a hotel.'

'Which hotel?' Swanker asked.

'This one,' Clive said.

A sudden transformation came over Mrs Swanker.

'Did I hear you correctly, boys? Did you say your father is the manager of this hotel? The Hotel Royal?'

'That's right,' Clive said. 'He's acting manager for six weeks, and while he's here, we're living in a humbug.'

'Suite, Clive!' I reminded.

'A suite? Your father is the manager here, and you have a suite?'

'Yeah,' Clive drawled. 'As a matter of fact, we're all living in the doss-house suite.'

'Penthouse suite, Clive,' I said, giving him a nudge.

'Yeah, penthouse. Up on the top. You can see St Paul's from where we are.'

'St Paul's what?' Swanker asked.

'St Paul's Cathedral,' Clive said.

'So what are *you* doing here then, Swank?' I said. 'Are you on your hols?'

Mrs Swanker Watson cleared her throat daintily and said, 'We are here on a short cultural vacation, actually, boys,' she said. 'We wanted to show Horace' – which is Swanker's real name – 'his cultural heritage, to show him the fine art and culture which makes London one of the most outstanding cities in the world.'

'Ah, right,' Clive said. 'So you'll be going to the Hard Rock Café and the Chamber of Horrors then, will you?'

Mrs Swanker muttered something then. I don't know if I heard her rightly, but it sounded as if she said, 'Why go all the way to the Chamber of Horrors to see waxworks, when you can see little living horrors right in front of you?'

But I might have misheard.

'We're hoping to go up the London Nose with our dad,' Clive said.

'London Eye,' I explained.

'How nice,' Mrs Swanker said. 'Well, we mustn't keep you.'

'That's all right,' Clive said. 'We're in no hurry.'

'Well, we are, I'm afraid,' Mr Swanker said. 'We've had no dinner yet. And I've had nothing to drink for weeks. But I suddenly feel the need to. So if you'll excuse us.'

'Oh, righto,' Clive said. 'How's the pool?'

'Great,' said Swanker.

'You didn't do any wees in it, did you?' Clive asked.

'Certainly not!' Mrs Swanker said. 'The very idea! Horace would never dream of such a thing.'

Clive gave me a look. Mrs Swanker plainly hadn't heard about the sad and unfortunate business during the school swimming gala then.

'Well, we'll have to get together,' Swanker said. 'We're here for a week.'

'Right you are, Swank,' I said. 'What room are you in?'

'We don't know,' Mrs Swanker said. 'It varies. Horace will find you.'

'Oh – OK. We can find your room anyway. Our dad'll know, being the manager.'

'We might be out.'

'We'll wait till you come back,' Clive said. 'No probs. See you later then, Swank.'

'Yeah, see you later, you two,' Swanker said, and off they all went.

We watched them go.

'Funny, you know, Clive,' I said. 'I don't know if you felt this, but I definitely had the sense that although old Swanker was pleased to see us, his mum and dad weren't quite so keen.'

'Nah,' Clive said. 'They looked dead chuffed to me. I mean, us being here, it's company for old Swanker, isn't it? He won't have to be on his ownsome, doing boring stuff. He can hang around with us and they can get him off their hands.'

The Swanker Watsons went on down the corridor. I heard Mr Swanker call to a porter. 'Could you get me a bottle of Scotch and bring it up to my room!' he said.

'Is that wise, dear?' Mrs Swanker said to him.

He stopped at the end of the corridor and looked back to where Clive was standing.

'Yes,' he said. 'It is.'

Then they disappeared from sight.

8

The Waxworks

We didn't see a whole lot of Dad for those first few days at the Hotel Royal, and not much of him after. For a time, as I shall be explaining soon, we saw nothing of him whatsoever. In fact we didn't think we would be seeing him ever again.

The job of hotel manager is a busy one which never seems to stop. Most people go home from work in the evenings, but when a hotel manager lives in the very hotel he is managing, he never really goes home at all. The result is that even when he is off-duty, he still gets calls from the front desk, asking him to deal with all the emergencies.

'I demand to see the manager.'

Irate guests – things like that.

'I don't wish to talk to you, my man, I wish to speak to the manager in person! Don't fob me off with excuses! Get me the manager this instant.'

It was always the same. Whenever somebody got upset about something, whenever they felt that their bill was wrong, or that they hadn't received good enough service in the restaurant, or that their bathroom towels hadn't been changed, they invariably wanted to speak to the manager.

Of course a hotel manager can't deal with all the minor problems all the time, especially when they are really small and trivial ones; he has to delegate. But if it was some regular customer who was complaining, or some famous film star, or someone who might bring bad publicity, Dad just had to go and sort it out himself.

People can be very touchy about the smallest things when they are paying a lot of money for them – and the Hotel Royal was very expensive. We could never have afforded to stay there, ever. The rooms were so pricey that we couldn't even have afforded a night in the broom cupboard. But there we were, just the same, living in the lap of luxury, and it wasn't costing us a penny.

From time to time, Mrs Dominics might ring up to see how things were going, or she would call in at the hotel for afternoon tea. She left Dad to get on with it mostly, though, and she seemed pleased with the way he was running things. She didn't actually stay at the hotel, as she had her own house in the country, a few miles outside London, along with plenty of other houses in cities all over the world.

Mrs Dominics is what is known as 'not short of a few bob'.

Now, because Dad was so busy, Clive and me had to more or less look after ourselves. To be honest, it was more along the lines of me looking after us both. Clive is not really up to looking after himself – because Clive is not actually a responsible person. Clive should be wearing L-plates really, as he is not yet fully competent to be in charge of a body – his. When it comes to being a human being, Clive has yet to pass his test, and sometimes I think he never will.

For our first few days at the Hotel Royal, we kept ourselves amused by visiting the swimming pool, the gym, the roof gardens, the garden restaurant, the Windsor restaurant, the Hot Muffin café, the Royal Bistro, and the Hotel Royal Tearooms.

It is my estimation that Clive managed to double his body weight in about a day and a half. If there is one thing that Clive is good at – and there aren't many – it is eating, and if there was ever an Olympic event called Stuffing Your Face Big Time, then Clive would win the gold medal hands down, and then he would probably eat it.

Of course, once we had exhausted the restaurants, there was always room service, and many a happy hour Clive and I spent up in our suite, working our way through the room service menu and watching the latest movies on the in-house cable channel on our big TV.

Unfortunately, Dad got wind of how much Clive was eating and he had to have a word with him about his big room service orders.

'Clive,' he said. 'I've been informed by the desk that in the few days we have been here you have already run up a room service bill of absolutely enormous proportions.'

'Wasn't me,' Clive said. But then he says that to everything.

'If it wasn't you, why do all these room service orders have your signature?'

Dad produced a wodge of room service bills, and sure enough, there was Clive's unmistakeable signature – a big X at the bottom of each one.

'I – I got peckish,' Clive said.

(I have to admit here that I had eaten quite a bit of room service myself, but I hadn't signed for anything. I'd got Clive to do that by telling him he was good at signing. Clive always falls for it when you tell him he is good at something.)

'Truffles?' Dad said, leafing through the bills. 'Ducks' eggs in aspic?'

'Didn't like them much,' Clive said.

'So what did you do with them?'

'Don't remember.'

'Chocolate milkshakes – two dozen?'

'Thirsty,' Clive said.

'Peas – one?'

'Thought I should have some vegetables.'

'From now on,' Dad said, 'no more room service. You can eat in the staff canteen. Someone has to pay for all this, you know. It's coming out of Mrs Dominics's profits. No more taking advantage, OK?'

'Sorry,' Clive said, and I think he meant it. We neither of us had added up what it would all cost. But this is the trouble with posh hotels, the simplest thing costs a fortune. Say you want an apple. Well, you can buy an apple in a shop for a few pence or so. But if you want room service to bring you an apple, by the time you have paid for someone to buy it, someone to wash it and someone to put it on a plate, and then put the plate on a silver salver, along with a napkin, a knife and a little finger bowl of water with a slice of lemon in it for cleaning your fingers with, and by the time you've paid for someone to bring it up to your room, the price of your apple has gone up to two hundred and seventeen pounds and sixty-five pence (plus tip).

That is why things are so expensive in hotels and why it is always best to bring your own apples. Bananas are just the same.

Because Dad was the manager, Clive and me got to explore behind the scenes as well as the bit the public saw. We even got a look in the kitchens of the Hotel Royal Grill, which is the best of its restaurants, with loads of awards and stars.

We didn't stay in there long though, because of

Gilbert Rimsey, the head chef. He is supposed to be the best chef in the country, but he is terrible at shouting, and when he clapped eyes on me and Clive he went ballistic.

'What are those ******* kids doing in my ******* kitchen?' he yelled. 'Get the little ***** out of here right now before I stick a wooden spoon up their ****s.'

Clive and I decided not to continue with our kitchen inspection then, but to turn our talents to places where they would be more appreciated, for Gilbert Rimsey did not just have an interesting vocabulary, he was also pretty good at throwing pans at people and not missing them.

Gilbert Rimsey was almost as famous for his swearing as he was for his cooking, so one of the porters said. Apparently he had studied swearing for many years, all over the world, with some of the best swearers there were. He had even gone to India and studied swearing with holy men and a bloke who lived in a thorn bush.

Personally I was not surprised that a bloke who lived in a thorn bush would know a lot about swearing. If I had to sleep in a thorn bush, I'd be swearing all the ******* time.

The porter went on to explain to us that Gilbert Rimsey had studied swearing in the kitchens of some of the best hotels in London, Paris and New York. He could swear in fourteen different languages –

and that was before he had even learnt how to boil an egg.

If you want to be a great chef, it is essential to study swearing before you start to cook, as you will get nowhere without it.

As far as cooking goes, swearing is known as the invisible ingredient, and if you ever cook a dish and it doesn't taste very good, all you have to do is stand and swear at it for a while, and that will liven it up no end. And if you ever have a customer who doesn't like his dinner, you just need to swear at him too, and he'll soon change his mind. If that doesn't work, you can always throw a pan at him.

Gilbert Rimsey had got several awards for his swearing, some of them very eminent indeed, and they were all pinned up in his kitchen. He had got a big rosette for inventing new swearwords and he was also included in *The Good Swearing Guide*.

Sometimes people would come from far and near to visit the Hotel Royal Grill restaurant just to hear him swearing, and they would not bother having a meal at all. They would just start off with a few light curses, then have a couple of courses of heavy cussing (vegetarian option available) and then round the meal off with a spot of abusive language, and that would do them nicely.

Gilbert Rimsey was the only chef in the country to have five stars for his cooking and seventeen stars for his language.

Well, after two or three days in the hotel, Dad could see that me and Clive were itching to get out and see a bit of London, like he had promised we would. Unfortunately, Dad simply didn't have the time to take us anywhere, but he decided that wouldn't stop us, and after giving as a long lecture on how to behave, he said he would give us some money and let us go out on our own, as we were probably old enough now.

He managed to get an hour off from managing the hotel and he took us to an Underground station and showed us how to buy tickets and to find our way around, so that we could be independent when we had our day out.

'Take the mobile phone with you,' he said. 'Give me a list of the places you're going to, so I'll know where you are and when you're supposed to be there. And look after each other.'

Of course what that meant was that I had to look after Clive.

We drew up a list of the places we wanted to visit and we set off the following morning armed with money, a phone, a list, a tube-train map, and a *London A to Z.*

'If you get lost,' Dad said, 'get a taxi and tell him to bring you here. Even if you don't have any money. I'll pay him when you arrive.'

So off we went. But just as we were leaving the hotel, we ran into the Swanker Watsons, who were milling around in the foyer.

'Pretend we haven't seen them,' I'm sure I heard Mrs Swanker Watson say, and I also thought I heard her mutter something about 'rough boys' and 'the gormless one and the idiot' but I was probably mistaken.

'Hiya, Swanker,' Clive said. 'What are you doing? Me and pie-face here' – that was a disrespectful reference to yours truly – 'are off out for the day. We're going to visit the waxworks and the London Contact Lens—'

'Eye,' I reminded him.

'And the zoo. And Buckingham Palace. And the Post Office Tower. And Trafalgar Square and Trafalgar Circle. And Nelson's Column. And Nelson's Gate. And Nelson's Compost Heap. And Nelson's Lawn Mower. And Nelson's Pencil Sharpener . . .' (Clive didn't really know where we were going at all.)

'Cor, great!' Swanker said.

'Why don't you come with us?' Clive said. 'After all, three's company, but two's a crowd.'

(I didn't think he'd got that quite right.)

Swanker looked at his mum and dad.

'Can I go with them?' he said. 'Can I? Please?'

'Well,' Mrs Swanker Watson demurred. 'We were going to visit the Tate art gallery . . .'

'Oh, you don't want to bother with boring old art galleries,' Clive said. 'Not when you come to London. No, you want to try and find a Mr

Softee van and get a bit of culture with a flake in it.'

'We're thinking of going to the Science Museum too, if we've time,' I said, so that Mrs Swanker wouldn't think we were total morons and all tarred with the same brush as Clive.

'Please, Mum . . .' Swanker said. I guessed that he was bored with hanging round with his parents, and maybe they also wanted a break from him. You always appreciate people more when you've had a break from them. I am hoping to get a nice long fifty-year break from Clive at some point, and then no doubt I will be able to see his finer qualities when we meet up again for the reunion.

'Well, I dare say you might prefer to be with people your own age for a while. What do you think, dear?'

'All the same to me,' Mr Swanker said. 'I suppose it would give me time to visit Burlington Arcade and buy a new hip flask.'

So Mr and Mrs Swanker decided to let Swanker go off with us.

'They are the manager's children, after all,' I heard Mrs Swanker say as we pushed our way through the revolving door and out into the fume-filled, traffic-filled, pedestrian-filled, noise-filled street. 'I'm sure he's keeping them on a tight rein and won't be letting them go rampaging all over the place. Nothing can go that wrong.'

We turned left and headed for the tube station.

We were going to the Waxworks.

The Waxworks were good, but they were really crowded. We didn't know who some of the celebrities were supposed to be, but others we recognized immediately. One of these was Daphne Spurter, the famous Hollywood actress who Clive is in love with.

Clive has been in love with her ever since he saw her on the telly in some film in which she fell in love with a bloke called Clive who had a wasting disease. (Clive also has a wasting disease, in that he wastes everything he gets his hands on – but that is not strictly speaking a medical condition.) At the end of this film, Daphne Spurter holds this bloke Clive's hand just as he is about to give the bucket a good kicking and she says, 'I love you. I love you, Clive. And I always will.'

Anyway, Clive, being Clive, got it into his head that all because Daphne Spurter loved some bloke called Clive in a film, then that meant she loved him too. He has trouble separating fact from fiction sometimes, especially when it comes to who ate the biscuits and his school reports.

'If I ever meet Daphne Spurter,' Clive said, looking at her waxwork, 'I'm going to marry her.'

'Marry her?' I said. 'She wouldn't marry you with a bargepole.'

'We're in love,' Clive said. 'If I had the money, I'd buy that waxwork and take it home and I'd keep her next to me always. Even in the bath.'

'She'd melt, wouldn't she?' Swanker Watson pointed out. 'In a hot bath.'

'I'd still love her,' Clive said. 'Even if she melted.'

'You could still have her as a candle, I suppose,' Swanker said.

'Bit big for a candle,' I said. 'And she doesn't have a wick that I can see.'

'I'd still love her,' Clive said. 'Even if she was just a blob.'

'If she was a blob, you'd be two of a kind then, wouldn't you?' I said. 'It would be a match made in heaven.'

But then Swanker spotted another figure.

'Here,' he said. 'Look at that. What do you reckon? Do you think that's a waxwork, or do you think it's alive?'

The figure was quite immobile, so it was hard to say.

'Well,' said Clive. 'There's one way to find out. Follow me and I'll show you how.'

Now, if you've ever been to the Waxworks, you will know that as well as the wax models of famous people from the past and present, and the gruesome figures in the Chamber of Horrors, there are also the attendants.

Some of the attendants keep themselves amused

by pretending to be waxworks. They stand stock-still and wait until people come up to them saying, 'Is that a waxwork?' and then they suddenly cough or sneeze or say 'Boo!' and they frighten the daylights out of you.

We had already had the daylights frightened out of us once by an attendant pretending to be a waxwork, so this time, Clive was taking no chances.

The figure in question was dressed in an attendant's uniform but had all the glassy pallor of wax. It didn't convince me though. I still thought it was a real person. It was a very big real person too, with quite a sizeable rear end.

'Five quid says it's a waxwork,' Clive said. 'And here goes to find out.'

Instead of approaching the figure from the front, as we'd done before, Clive took the sneaky way and crept up from behind, as Swanker and I watched. I guess we had both assumed that Clive was going to give the figure a little prod with his finger, or maybe even tickle it to see if it laughed. But no. That wasn't what Clive had in mind.

He sneaked up behind the immobile figure, swung back his foot, and gave it the most enormous kick right up the backside.

'Owwwwwwwwwwwww!'

I turned to Swanker Watson.

'See,' I said. 'I told you it wasn't a waxwork. That's five pounds Clive owes me.'

* * *

After they'd thrown us out of the Waxworks, we decided to take an open-topped bus tour of London. Unfortunately for Clive, he managed to get his recorded commentary stuck on to the Japanese channel, so he sat there with his earphones in, not understanding a word of what was going on. (Though to be honest, even if it had been in English, he probably wouldn't have made much sense of that either.)

When the bus came to the London Eye, the huge revolving wheel by the Thames, we got off and queued up for tickets to go up in one of the capsules. It took half an hour to get the tickets and half an hour to get on and half an hour to go all the way round. The views were fantastic though, and we really enjoyed it, although I'm not so sure that the other people in our capsule did, as Swanker Watson seemed to have had some baked beans with his breakfast and was now determined to share the experience with us all.

After that it was time for some lunch and then we got back on the open-topped bus and went round the rest of the circuit.

There was so much to see in London that though we stayed out all day we only saw a fraction of it.

'We'll have to come back tomorrow,' Clive said. 'We can't see it all in a day. Do you think it'll still be here in the morning?'

'Well, where's it going to go, Clive?' I said. 'It's a bit big to fold up and put away in a box. I don't think that all of London is going to disappear overnight.'

'I'm getting hungry again,' Clive said. 'Are you hungry, Swanker?'

It was an unnecessary question, for Swanker is like Clive, he is always hungry and probably has a tapeworm, maybe even two.

It was dusk by then. We got the tube-train to Piccadilly and walked back towards the hotel. All the neon lights were on everywhere. We took a detour through Leicester Square; it was teeming with people on their way to restaurants and cinemas and theatres, or just simply there to see the sights. It made our home town look small and provincial – but then I guess that's what it is.

We bought some ice-cream, and after that some pizza slices from one of the little hot-pizza kiosks, just to keep us going. They had huge pizzas on display, the size of car wheels, and they peeled you off a slice of the one you wanted. We walked on, munching steadily, and then we turned the corner into the road for our hotel.

'What the . . . ?'

We all skidded to a halt.

'What's going on?' Swanker said. 'What's happening? What are all those people doing there?'

Because there were hundreds of them, maybe thousands. They were all but blocking the street and the police were doing all they could to maintain some order and to keep the traffic flowing. And all the people were milling around the entrance to our hotel.

'Move aside there, please. Move aside.'

The hotel entrance was cordoned off with velvet ropes looped between metal stands. And leading all the way from the steps to the kerbside was one long, enormous red carpet.

'Wow!' Swanker said. 'Look. There must be someone famous coming to stay at the hotel.'

Clive was on his tiptoes, trying to see over people's heads, and getting all excited though he didn't know why – which is typical Clive.

'Who is it? What's going on?' he cried. 'What's everyone looking at? Can anyone lend me some money?'

Just then a car rounded the corner. It was a long stretch-limo with blacked-out windows. It was at least as long as a bus. In fact, it was so long, you wondered how it managed to get round corners at all. When it stopped, it probably took a good five minutes for the back of the car to catch up with the front.

'Who is it? Is it someone famous? Is it the Prime Minister? Is it Mrs Lippiat from our school? Is it that bloke from the telly who does the ads? Is it that girl from the whatdoyoucall it who does the thing? Is it that magician? Is it—' And then Clive, in his flurry and excitement, turned to me and he said something quite extraordinary. He said, 'Is it Mum?'

I could have cried. I could have sat down on the pavement and cried.

I don't often have tender feelings for Clive, but I did then.

'No, Clive,' I said. 'It's not Mum, I'm afraid.'

'N-no,' he said. 'I-I didn't really think so . . . I just thought – for a minute – in the excitement – that it might – have been – that everyone was waiting for – that it – might have been – Mum.'

'I wish it was, Clive,' I said. 'I wish it was.'

'Yeah,' he said. 'Me too.'

Then he turned back round and went on shouting, like it had never happened.

'Who is it?' he yelled. 'Is it the Beatles? Is it Elvis? Is it Cleopatra? Is it Henry the Eighth?'

A woman turned and gave him a nasty look.

'For heaven's sake,' she said. 'Will you stop shouting in my ear?'

'Well, do you know who it is then?' Clive said. 'Could you tell us, please?'

'Honestly,' the woman said. 'Kids today. Don't you ever watch the news or read the papers?'

'Not if I can help it,' Clive said. 'It's too depressing.'

'Who is it please, madam?' Swanker said. 'Do you know?'

Right then the stretch-limo swooshed to a halt, its

passenger door level with the red carpet. The hotel doorman hurried to open the door. He was holding an umbrella, though it wasn't raining.

As the car door opened, a fusillade of flashlights went off, as the photographers milling around the steps used their cameras. TV crews surged forwards, trying to get a good view and a good angle and maybe a few words.

'Who is it? Is it a band? Is it a film star?'

Then a blond-haired, slender woman got out of the car, accompanied by the most enormous minder you have ever seen. She smiled and waved to the crowd for a moment, before being hurried into the safety and the protection of the hotel lobby.

'Oh my,' Clive said. 'Oh my, it's her. She's come for me.'

I just managed to catch him as he fainted to the ground and as the blond-haired lady vanished into the hotel.

It was Daphne Spurter, the film star.

She looked almost as convincing as her waxwork.

I just hoped that Clive didn't get it into his head to try checking out that she was real.

9

Daphne Spurter

'Fetch a bucket of water, Swanker,' I said. 'And throw it over Clive. That'll soon bring him round.'

'Good idea,' Swanker Watson said willingly (as he is quite keen on emergencies). 'In fact, why don't I get two buckets? Or maybe even a fire hose?'

'Smart thinking, Swanker,' I said. 'And maybe, while you're getting that, you might be able to borrow some kind of electric-shock machine. We could get poor Clive here wired up to that and it'll have him back on his feet in no time. It's a well-known fact that two hundred volts is as good as an aspirin any day.'

Clive's eyes opened.

'Hello,' he said. 'Where am I? Who are you? What's going on? Who's that fat ugly boy with a face like mushy peas?'

'That's Swanker,' I said.

'No, that's your brother,' Swanker told him.

'I've just had the most beautiful dream,' Clive said, sitting up on the pavement. 'I dreamt I saw a vision of loveliness.'

'What?' said Swanker. 'You mean you saw a double cheeseburger with fries?'

'No,' Clive said. 'I saw the girl of my dreams – Daphne Spurter, the star of stage, screen and moving picture. And she was right there in front of me. And she waved and smiled. And then it all went dark.'

'Get up, Clive,' I said. 'You'll make the pavement dirty. It wasn't a dream. You did see her. We all did. She's staying at our hotel by the look of it.'

Clive scrambled to his feet and dusted himself off.

'Then what are we waiting for?' he said. 'Let's get in and have a look at her. We might get an autograph.' And then he went all moony and soppy looking. 'We might even get – a peck on the cheek.'

'Clive,' I said, 'it would be a brave bird that would risk pecking your cheeks. The only thing that would peck your cheeks would be a territorially-minded ostrich. And it wouldn't be the cheeks on your face it would be pecking either.'

'Come on,' said Swanker. 'We might catch her at the check-in desk.'

The crowds were dispersing from outside the hotel now, and the red carpet was being rolled away. But a few dozen people still lingered, in the hopes of blagging their way inside, or of glimpsing their idol when she came out again.

'I wonder what she's doing here,' Clive said, as we made our way to the Hotel Royal revolving door. 'She's a long way from Hollywood.'

'Maybe she's come here to do some shopping,' Swanker opined. 'Film stars are always shopping.'

'Could be,' Clive said. 'I noticed a branch of Tesco round the corner. Maybe she's flown over to get a few oven pads and some pop-tarts.'

'Don't be stupid, Clive,' I said. 'No one's going to fly ten thousand miles for a pop-tart.'

'I would,' Clive said.

But then it is a well-known fact that Clive would crawl to the north pole on his hands and knees for a free pop-tart; he'd probably even do it for peanuts.

'What do you lot want? This hotel isn't for scruffbags.'

The usual hotel doorman – Michael – had been temporarily reinforced with an immense bouncer in a dark suit wearing a name badge reading *Wiggles*. He was probably there for the duration of Daphne Spurter's stay. His white shirt was about the size of the mainsail on a yacht.

Clive took umbrage at being called a scruffbag. I can't think why, as the poor man was only speaking the truth.

'How dare you, my man!' Clive said, getting all hoity-toity. 'I'll have you know that we are staying at this hotel and have contacts in high places. So stand aside and let us pass, before I summon the servants to set the dogs on you and get the groom to come and give you a horse-whipping.'

The bouncer gave Clive a curious look, as if he were thinking of picking him up and dumping him in the litter bin, after first pulling his ears off and putting them in his pockets to make sure he was tidy.

'It's all right, Wiggy,' Mike the hotel doorman said. 'They *are* staying here, believe it or not, all three of them. You can let them in.'

'Thanks, Mike,' I said.

'No problem, lads,' he answered. So the three of us went inside. Unfortunately, we were so anxious to get away from the bouncer that we all three managed to get into the same segment of the revolving door. We immediately got stuck.

'Clive,' I said, 'what are you doing?'

'What are *you* doing?' he said.

'Swanker,' I said. 'What are you doing?'

'Trying to breathe,' he said. 'What else?'

Unable to move, we hammered on the glass panel of the revolving door, while Swanker did dying goldfish impressions with his eyeballs. Wiggles the bouncer saw us before Mike did. He was over in a couple of strides, looking suspiciously gleeful and over-willing to help.

'Allow me, lads!' he said. 'Are you stuck?' And with that he got hold of the revolving door with both of his paws and he gave it a huge shove. 'There,' he said. 'That'll free it.'

The door spun round and we got thrown out of it at about fifty miles an hour. Swanker ended up in a big plant pot; I landed on a luggage trolley, and Clive slid halfway across the polished lobby floor before coming to a halt by something that looked like an old spittoon. When he hit it with his head, it sounded like someone banging a gong.

'You all right, Clive?' I asked.

But he wasn't interested in his injuries.

'Look,' he said. 'There she is. And look who she's with!'

And sure enough, there was Daphne Spurter, the famous Hollywood actress, surrounded by her entourage, all standing by the check-in desk. And who was she talking to? Who was making her welcome? Who was saying how delighted he was to have her here and shaking her by the hand?

Our dad. That was who.

'Come on,' Clive said. 'Quick.'

We wormed our way through the crowd of hangers-on.

'And anything we can do for you, Miss Spurter,' Dad was saying, 'in any way at all . . .'

'Well,' she drawled, in a strong American accent, 'there is one thing. My jewels . . .'

'Your jewels?'

'The hotel has a safe? I mean, not like a little

111

room safe, but a real, secure, big burglar-proof safe?'

'We do indeed. In my office.'

'Maybe I could deposit some things.'

'Certainly. Now?'

'Why not.'

'This way, please.'

'Hiya Dad. Who's your friend? Is she staying for the evening? Will she be wanting to borrow one of your shirts and use the spare toothbrush like the other ladies do?'

'Oh . . .'

Dad blushed. Daphne Spurter and her entourage looked down at Clive – who had been the one to speak – and then at me and at Swanker.

'Oh, good heavens!' Daphne Spurter said. 'Mr Johnson. Are these three yours?'

'N-no, Miss Spurter, just, eh, these two. And this is a friend of theirs.'

'Well, how are you boys?' Miss Spurter said. 'Nice to meet you.'

I thought Clive was going to float away. He had this daft-looking, rapt expression on his face. It's the kind of expression you sometimes see on the faces of babies in prams – a sort of expression of complete happiness and content. It's usually followed by somebody saying: 'I think that baby needs its nappy changed.'

'Nice to meet you too, Miss Spurter,' I said.

'Hello,' Swanker said. 'How you doing, baby?

What say we hit the clubs sometime and paint this town purple?' And he left it at that. (Just as well too, in my opinion.)

'*Ga-ga* . . .' Clive said. Only he never did get any further than that. Dad and Daphne Spurter disappeared into the manager's office, along with her personal assistant, who was carrying a slim leather case which must have contained the jewellery.

'Sh-she spoke to me,' Clive said, after she had gone. 'She spoke to me. She spoke with her voice into my very ears.'

'What else would she speak into? Your foot?'

'I think she's in love with me,' Clive said. 'Did you see how she looked at me? I think she wants to marry me.'

'Nobody wants to marry you, Clive,' I reminded him. 'There might be a few people who'd like to bury you. But marriage – I don't think so. And especially not with a Hollywood starlet.'

But he wasn't listening.

'She smiled at me,' Clive kept saying. 'It must be love.'

Just then there was a small commotion as Mrs Swanker Watson appeared.

'Horace,' she said. 'Did I just see you talking to that film star?'

'Oh, yeah,' Swanker said. 'Clive's dad introduced us.'

Mrs Swanker beamed at Clive and me.

'Well, well,' she said. 'Just fancy. I always said, Horace, that you should see more of Clive and his brother. Especially now that their father is the manager of the Hotel Royal. Where is your father now, boys?'

'He's locking Daphne Spurter in the strong-box for safe-keeping,' Clive said.

But this is Clive all over for you. He gets things half right and then he messes up the rest.

'I think Clive means he's putting her jewellery in the strong-box.'

'Ah, good,' Mrs Swanker said. 'Just what I came down to see him about myself. I need him to look after my diamonds.'

I noticed that she was carrying a leather case too. She probably didn't want to be outdone in the jewellery stakes by any starlets from Hollywood.

'I thought I'd better have these put in a safe place until I need to wear them. I'll need them again for tomorrow night, when Horace's father and I are going out for the evening.'

'Where are you going?' Clive asked. 'Ten-pin bowling? Or is it the bingo?'

Mrs Swanker gave Clive one of her weedkiller looks.

'Clive,' she said, 'one hardly wears one's diamonds to go ten-pin bowling, does one? One wears one's diamonds when one is going to the opera.'

'Ah, right,' Clive said. 'Gotcha.'

'Mum,' Swanker said. 'What's she doing here, do you know – Daphne Spurter?'

'Well,' Mrs Swanker Watson said, 'I'd imagine she's here for the premiere of her latest film – her new blockbuster, in which she plays a private detective tracking down a serial poisoner. I always read the society and the gossip columns, so I know about these things.'

'What's the film's title?' I asked. 'Do you know?'

'I believe it's called *Never Eat A Green Banana*,' Mrs Swanker said.

'Cor,' Clive said. 'Sounds chilling.'

'They're showing it at the Leicester Square cinema on Thursday night, I understand,' Mrs Swanker said. 'Though I never imagined that Daphne Spurter would be staying here in this very hotel. The same one as us!'

And then a thought lit up her whole frame. It was a thought of great swanking and of outdoing others. It was a thought of such swanking that if she achieved it she would never be out-swanked by anyone again. If she could only accomplish what she had in mind, then the gold cup for swanking would be hers for ever, an imperishable trophy, to sit permanently upon her mantelpiece. *Mrs Swanker Watson*, it would say, *World Champ and the Tops for Swanking. Queen of all the Swankers.*

She turned the whole force of her size-fourteen

smile upon me and Clive. When Mrs Swanker Watson does smiling, you don't forget it. There's probably about twenty thousand pounds' worth of dental work in there. In fact Mrs Swanker Watson's teeth are probably worth more than some people's houses.

I noticed that Clive had put his sunglasses on.

'Dear boys,' she said. 'I wonder. As you are such tremendous friends with Horace . . .'

I didn't know about tremendous. I mean, Swanker was all right, but it wasn't as if we were bosom buddies. The main thing we liked about Swanker was that he was handy with his wallet.

'. . . it would be so nice of you if you could have a word with your father and see if there are any tickets available for the premiere of Daphne Spurter's film. I'd so love to go to a premiere. The cars, the photographers, the television cameras, the fame. Everyone at home, all the neighbours, all seeing us on the TV – not that such things are of any importance to me personally, of course – but if you could, dear boys, have a word with your father, well, I'm sure that your kindness . . . wouldn't go unrewarded.'

Then she winked.

I looked at Clive and he looked at me. He took his dark glasses off so I could see him better.

She was offering us a bribe.

I could tell that Clive was torn. If anyone should

be going to premieres of films starring Daphne Spurter, then it ought to have been Clive. But realistically, there was no way Clive and me were ever going to get invited. Clive was never going to get in, not even if he borrowed Mrs Swanker's diamonds and evening dress and wore them with his best T-shirt – the one with *One Foot In The Bucket* on the front (which is the name of Clive's favourite band). The film was probably for grown-ups only anyway. And money was money, after all.

'We'll see,' I said, before Clive could answer, 'what we can do.' I decided that was the most tactful thing to say. 'But, to be honest, I doubt there's much even Dad can do to get a ticket. But I will ask.'

'Oh, thank you,' Mrs Swanker said. 'What nice boys you are. I must go and have a word with the desk clerk then, about depositing my jewellery.'

She gave us another blast of her mega-smile. It was a bit like a spotlight really, one of those ones you see lighting up the sky in old war films. Then she went over to see about her jewellery.

'Hey, Swanker,' Clive said. 'What's your mum's jewellery worth?'

'I dunno,' Swanker said. 'Few bob, I guess.'

'Is it worth more than her teeth?' Clive asked.

But Swanker wasn't listening, for Daphne Spurter had re-emerged from the manager's office, and Dad was seeing her out.

'Don't you worry, Miss Spurter,' Dad said. 'Your

valuables will be completely safe with us. There's only one person knows the combination – and I won't be telling anybody else.'

'Thank you, Mr Johnson,' she drawled. 'Now perhaps you'd care to show me to my suite?'

Well, normally, that was a porter's job, but when you have a Hollywood film star as a guest, it's down to the manager.

'Of course,' Dad said. 'This way.'

He snapped his fingers to get the attention of a couple of porters and indicated that they should follow with Daphne Spurter's luggage. Then they all set off towards the lift – Dad, Daphne Spurter, her luggage, the porters, and her entourage. She swept past us in a cloud of glamour and expensive scent. She certainly was pretty, I have to say that. I could see why Clive was in love with her, even if she was a bit old for him.

She'd have made a great mum though.

For those who didn't have one.

'Clive!' I said, waving my hand in front of his eyes, trying to break the spell. 'Clive, she's gone!'

'Oh has she?' he said. 'I thought I could still see her.'

'Come on,' I said. 'Let's go get our swimming stuff and have a dip in the pool. You coming, Swanker?'

So we all got our things and we headed for the health spa, down in the hotel basement.

I guess, looking back now, that we had already

started to take things too much for granted – all the luxury, and the room service, and the five star comforts and the swimming pool and the steam room. I loved that steam room. You could sit in there, slowly poaching, as if you were lost in the middle of a warm, damp fog.

Yes, it's amazing how quickly you get used to things, to high-living and to taking everything for granted. You think it's just going to go on for ever and never stop. It never crosses your mind that you could suddenly lose it all, in a matter of moments. No, you just go on sleepwalking through this cosseted and pampered, candyfloss world of luxury, where there aren't any sharp edges to hurt you at all.

And then suddenly you bump into something unexpected, and you get a rude awakening.

10

A Grilling

Daphne Spurter wasn't the only celebrity to arrive at the Hotel Royal that day.

As Clive, me, and Swanker Watson returned from the pool, dressed in deep-pile hotel dressing gowns and dripping water on the carpets, we saw two of the skinniest blokes we had ever seen, plus two of the fattest, all wearing dark glasses and weird-looking clothes, standing by the check-in desk.

'Hey, look,' Swanker said. 'Do you know who that is?'

'Is it the first arrivals for the Eating Disorders Society conference?'

'It's *Death Around The Corner*,' Swanker said. 'The heavy metal thrash punk garage hip-hop house rock blues soul funk and handbag band.'

'What sort of music do they play?' I asked.

'Loud mostly,' Swanker said.

'Hey, I've heard of them,' Clive said. 'They're far out.'

They certainly looked it. If they'd been any further out, they'd probably have had no chance of ever getting back in again.

'We'll see some fun now they're here,' Clive said.

'Oh,' I said. 'And why's that?'

'Rock band,' Clive said, in his don't-be-so-stupid-don't-you-know-anything tone.

'So?' I said.

'Well, you know,' he said. 'Rock band.'

'So?'

'Well, they get up to stuff.'

'Like what?'

'You know. They do mad stuff, like sawing the beds in half, or painting the room red, or throwing the TV out the window, or they order cream buns from room service then have bun fights, or they tie the waiter to the trouser press and cover him in shaving foam.'

'What for?' I said.

'A laugh,' Clive said.

'I see,' I said.

'Oh yes,' Clive said. 'It's great when you're in a rock band. In fact that's what I'm going to do when I leave school. I'm going to join a rock band and throw the telly out the window.'

'But what if your favourite programme's on?' I said.

'Well, you watch it first, then you throw the telly out of the window afterwards,' Clive said. 'I would have thought that was obvious. Don't you know anything about music?'

The four members of *Death Around The Corner* finished checking in at the reception desk and a porter loaded their bags onto a trolley.

'Say, fella,' one of the skinny ones said to the receptionist. Swanker said he was the lead singer, called Otis Carnage. 'Can I order something here?'

Clive nudged me with his elbow.

'Here we go,' he said. 'Wait for this. He'll want seventeen bottles of whisky, an axe, a chain saw, and a case of explosives.'

'Yes, sir. What would you like?' the receptionist asked.

'A pot of Earl Grey tea and a scone,' Otis said.

I looked at Clive.

'A pot of Earl Grey tea and a scone! He's not going to do much damage with that.'

'You wait,' Clive said. 'That's just for starters. You wait until he's had his tea. We'll see some fireworks then. I bet he'll throw his teabag out the window and then there'll be a riot.'

But I don't think Otis Carnage could have thrown his teabag out of the window, as there was no riot at all. In fact the last I saw of him was him sitting in a corner of the lobby, with a teapot on the table in front of him, doing the crossword in the evening paper.

No. It wasn't Otis Carnage and *Death Around The Corner* who caused the trouble that night.

It was Clive.

We were up in our suite at the time, looking at the room service menu and wondering what to have for dinner.

'I think I might have half a dozen hard-boiled quail's eggs,' Clive said, 'followed by a meat pie on the half shell and a cheesy dip, followed by a bag of Maltesers and some deep-fried crumpets. How does that sound?'

'Shouldn't you have something green with that?' I said.

'OK,' Clive said. 'I'll order green crumpets.'

Just then Dad came in to change his shirt. When you're the manager of a posh hotel, you have to change your shirt at least twice daily. Sometimes Dad changed his suit two or three times a day as well. Not that it mattered, as the laundry was done by the hotel on the premises.

'Clive,' he said. 'Put that room service menu down. I told you to lay off that. You two can eat in the staff canteen tonight.'

'But Dad—'

'But Dad nothing. I don't want the hotel employees getting fed up thinking you two are receiving special treatment. So you can go down and eat with everyone else. There's a great selection of food.'

'All right then,' Clive said. 'I don't mind.'

Dad put a fresh shirt on. 'Did you have a good day?'

'Great,' I said.

'See much of London?'

'Quite a bit.'

'Oh, Dad . . .' Clive said.

'Yes, Clive?'

'I don't suppose you'd be able to get Swanker's mum two tickets for the premiere of Daphne Spurter's film, would you?'

Dad put in his cufflinks. It was a proper shirt he was wearing, with no buttons on the sleeves. The cufflinks looked really smart.

'I'll ask,' he said. 'But I can't promise anything. Oh, and Clive . . .'

'Dad?'

'Next time you see Daphne Spurter, try not to stare at her so much. I think she finds having you stare at her a bit unnerving. She probably gets enough of being stared at out in the street. She might like a break from it while she's in the hotel.'

'I was only looking,' Clive said.

'Well, you were looking a bit like a lovesick cow,' Dad said. 'See you both later. I've got to rush. Bye.'

Personally I would have had Clive down as a

lovesick wart hog rather than a lovesick cow, but no doubt it is all in the eye of the beholder.

Martine the maid came in then to turn the beds down and to put a little chocolate on the pillow. She was Spanish and spoke English with a strong foreign accent, but she seemed to like Clive and me, and she always left us two chocolates each on our pillows, instead of the usual one, which was all that everyone else got.

'*Buenas noches*, boys,' she said, as she left.

'*Hasta la vista*, Martine,' Clive said. (Which is something he picked up from watching *Terminator* movies. He also scratches himself a lot, but I don't know which movie he picked that up from.)

'Come on then, Clive,' I said. 'Down for dinner in the staff canteen. Leave the chocolates for later.'

So down we went in our own private lift, all the way down to the basement. We followed the smell of dinner to the staff canteen, got some trays and heaped up the nourishment onto our plates.

Only Clive went and spilt some gravy onto the floor by our table.

And that was when the trouble started.

'Clive,' I said. 'You're back to your sloppy eating habits. You ought to get that gravy mopped up before somebody walks by, slips on it, and does themselves an injury.'

'Always nagging,' Clive said. 'Just because you think you're the eldest, but you're not. You're always going on. It's "Clive this" and it's "Clive that" and it's "Clive put the kettle on" and "Clive put the cat out".'

To the best of my knowledge I had never said 'Clive put the kettle on', for I would never have trusted Clive with hot liquids, as he is dangerous enough with cold ones.

'I'll mop it up in a minute,' Clive said, 'with a piece of bread.'

Before he did though, two of the waiters who worked in the Hotel Royal Grill walked by with their dinners on trays, getting a bit of sustenance in before the evening's work started. We sort of knew them by sight, as they were brothers like us – Paulo and Antonio, both from Italy. They were quite small, in fact not much taller than me and Clive, and they were dressed in white jackets, white shirts with bow ties, black trousers and black shiny shoes.

It was Paulo who stepped in the gravy and who went flying first. He landed on top of Antonio.

'Ahh! My-a-arm!'

'Ahh! My-a-ankle!'

Well, the upshot was that one had twisted his ankle and the other had sprained his wrist, and they were both out of action for the night.

'What-a stupid-a idiot left-a the gravy on-a the floor!' Paulo yelled out.

I didn't say anything. I knew who had done it, but I'm not one to grass anyone up – not even Clive, though it was tempting.

'Search me,' Clive said, feigning innocence – as he has done for several years now. 'But if you ever find out who it is, you ought to go for compensation. It's negligence that sort of thing. In fact, if I were you, I'd sue the manager.'

I kicked Clive under the table.

'Clive,' I reminded him, 'Dad's the manager.'

'When I said manager,' Clive said, 'I meant you ought to sue the cleaners, who should have mopped that gravy up.'

Paulo and Antonio limped and hobbled off to get their injuries seen to. Clive and I got rid of the gravy with some paper napkins, so as to destroy any evidence in the event of a prosecution.

The next thing we knew, Paulo and Antonio were back from first aid, wearing appropriate supports and bandages. They went over to a table where Gilbert Rimsey, the famous chef, was sitting plotting his menus.

'I'm-a sorry, Mr Rimsey,' Paulo said, flaunting his bandage, 'but me and-a my brother can't-a work tonight.'

Gilbert Rimsey took one look at him and went ballistic.

'What do you mean you can't ******* work tonight! Who's going to collect the ******* dishes from off the ******* tables in my ******* restaurant?'

'I don't-a know, Mr Rimsey.'

'Don't know! Don't ******* know! Well, you'd better ******* find out, you ******. Or I'll chop your ******** off, cook them to a crisp in the frier, and then stick them up your ********.'

Which all sounded a bit on the painful side to me, but I didn't like to get involved.

'What exactly did you do to yourselves?' Gilbert Rimsey demanded, managing for once to complete a whole sentence without a swearword in it.

Paulo pointed towards where we were sitting.

'We-a slipped, on some gravy.'

Gilbert Rimsey flashed a look across at us.

'You!' he said. 'You two! You spilt that gravy. I ******* saw you earlier. You're responsible for this! Who the **** do you think you are!'

Clive was shaking a little by then and getting ready to run, and I was getting ready to follow him. Gilbert Rimsey was up on his feet and bearing down upon us.

'Well?' he said. 'Are you ******* deaf or something?'

'N-no, Mr Rimsey,' Clive said. 'W-we're related to the m-manager. He's our dad.'

'Listen, pea-brain,' Gilbert Rimsey said to Clive (which showed, to my mind, that despite his use of strong language, he was a shrewd judge of character). 'I don't care who you're related to. I don't care if the Pope's your dad.'

'I d-don't think the Pope's married,' Clive said.

'And if he is our dad, we've never had a birthday card from him.'

'You've nobbled my bus-boys,' Gilbert Rimsey said. 'And as they can't work in the Grill tonight – you'll have to do their jobs for them.'

'But I'm too young to drive a bus,' Clive protested. 'I don't even have a licence. The only licence I've got is from driving a little electric car at Legoland.'

'Yeah, and even then you failed on your first attempt,' I reminded him.

'Don't be stupid,' Gilbert Rimsey said. 'A bus-boy doesn't drive a ******* bus! He wheels a trolley around and discreetly collects the used plates and cutlery from off the tables. Now, I'm sure even a couple of ******* retards like you two can manage that.'

'What's a retard?' Clive asked.

'Take a look in the mirror later on, Clive,' I said. 'If you're lucky, you might see one.' I turned to Gilbert Rimsey then and faced him square on. He wasn't going to intimidate me and Clive. Not when we had connections in high places.

'Now see here, Mr Rimsey,' I said. 'Me and Clive here happen to be important personages in this hotel, and if our dad, the acting manager, finds out that—'

I never got to finish.

'If your dad finds out that you've crippled two of my waiters, and you've wrecked the smooth

130

running of my ******* restaurant on the very night when I've got Daphne ******* Spurter eating there along with the cream of showbiz society, I don't think that your dad is going to be all that happy. Not when the reputation of my restaurant goes down the plughole and this hotel's reputation goes down with it.'

I could see there was a certain truth in that.

'But if you do the job for tonight, I shan't tell him,' he said.

'He might come into the Grill and see us,' I pointed out.

'He might, but he probably won't even notice you. He's not expecting to see you, and a good waiter is almost invisible. You borrow Paulo and Antonio's jackets and ties, you smarm your hair down with a dollop of gel, and no one'll know the difference. Just one night, that's all I'm asking.'

Gilbert Rimsey leant forwards, then he lowered his voice and grew confidential.

'But if you don't do it, lads,' he said, 'I shall have your guts for ******* garters!'

I have to admit that Gilbert Rimsey was a very persuasive man. There are some people who cannot make you budge in your opinions at all. But Gilbert Rimsey definitely had the gift of the gab. Or maybe it was more the gift of the large knuckles. Either way, he could talk you into stuff.

'Well, Clive,' I said. 'What do you think?'

But Clive had gone all moony-faced and starry-eyed again.

'Daphne Spurter,' he said. 'You mean – I'd get to clear her table? I'd get to touch the very fork she had in her hands? The very straw she drank her soup with? The very knife she used for sticking in her bread roll? The very plate she licked the gravy from?'

Gilbert Rimsey plainly did not share Clive's star-struck view of Daphne Spurter's table manners, but then Gilbert Rimsey was probably not fazed by celebrities, being a bit of a one himself.

'Yes. Something like that,' he said.

'Then show me the uniform,' Clive said. 'Show me the way to my bus.'

'The Grill restaurant,' Gilbert Rimsey said. 'One hour. And don't be late!'

So it was that one hour later, Clive and I, dressed in uniforms borrowed from Paulo and Antonio, presented ourselves at the Hotel Royal Grill to start work for the evening.

We had taken the precaution of not removing Paulo and Antonio's name badges from their jackets. We felt that it was best for us to remain incognito, in the unlikely event of any trouble.

The head waiter, Monsieur Philippe, looked at us with a jaundiced eye.

'So,' he said. 'You nobbled my two best bus-boys.'

'Don't worry about it,' Clive said. 'Why worry about bus-boys when you can have taxi-boys!'

Monsieur Philippe didn't seem much impressed. He obviously thought that if Clive was a taxi-boy, then he was probably some kind of clapped-out minicab. In my opinion Clive was more of a horse-and-cart boy.

'OK,' Monsieur Philippe said. 'There're your trolleys. Just keep your eyes peeled and when you see that someone has finished a course, you discreetly approach them, you discreetly remove the dirty plates and cutlery, and you discreetly wheel the dishes away into the kitchen. And you do it all discreetly. Got it?'

'Got it,' I said. 'Discreetly – right, Clive?'

'Right,' he said. Then he paused a second and added: 'What was it again?'

'Discreetly!' Monsieur Philippe snapped.

'It comes back to me now,' Clive said. 'I remember, thanks.'

'And whatever you do,' Monsieur Philippe said, 'you don't bother the guests, OK? You don't talk to the diners. You don't make eye contact with them. As far as they're concerned, you don't even exist. You're a nothing. You're a nobody, got that?'

'You shouldn't have any problems with that, should you, Clive?' I said. 'You're quite used to being a nothing and a nobody, eh?'

Clive gave me a nasty look.

'**** off,' he said.

Monsieur Philippe looked shocked.

'Where did a boy of your age pick up language like that?' he said.

'Gilbert ******* Rimsey,' Clive explained.

'Ah,' Monsieur Philippe said, nodding sadly, and he went off to greet some diners. 'Good evening, good evening, so very nice to see you – welcome. We have a table for you here by the window.'

It was Mr and Mrs Swanker Watson. Swanker wasn't with them though. They must have left him in the room with the TV and some room service.

'Well, dear,' I overheard Mrs Swanker say as Monsieur Philippe showed her and Mr Swanker to their table. 'This looks nice. A lovely place to celebrate our anniversary.'

'Yes,' Mr Swanker said – though he didn't sound all that happy about it. 'We must have a few bottles of champagne to celebrate.'

'Must we?' Mrs Swanker said, a note of concern in her voice.

'Yes,' Mr Swanker insisted. 'We must!' And he beckoned for the wine waiter to come over.

While Mr and Mrs Swanker were waiting for the champagne to arrive, Clive went and took their glasses away.

'Did that waiter look at all familiar to you?' Mrs Swanker said.

'Who? The one with the smarmed down hair

134

and the name badge saying *Paulo*?' Mr Swanker asked.

'Yes.'

'Umm, vaguely. They all look the same though really, don't you think?'

'I wonder why he took our glasses away.'

'Maybe they were a bit dusty.'

Monsieur Philippe saw what Clive had done and he bore down upon him, just as Clive started clearing another table.

'What are you doing!' he demanded.

'I'm being a bus-boy and doing bus-boy stuff, like you said,' Clive told him.

'*Dirty* glasses and plates!' Monsieur Philippe said. 'Not *clean* ones! Put it all back.'

'All right. All right. No need to be so ******* touchy,' Clive said.

I could see that I was going to have to speak to Clive about his language.

Clive and me didn't have much to do for the first hour, and to be honest, it was quite good fun being a bus-boy and being on the other side of the table, as it were, so to speak.

Sitting in a restaurant as a customer is one thing, but when you work there, you see people in a different light: you see all their affectations and pretensions, their airs and graces and their insecurities; you see the way they look around the dining room at each other, wondering who's got more money, or if they're looking at somebody famous that they ought to know. Whereas to them, you're just part of the furniture – the chairs, the tables, the potted plants, the bus-boy.

At about half past eight, Daphne Spurter arrived with a few close friends. Everyone in the restaurant had a good look at them while pretending not to stare. They settled down at a table, with Monsieur Philippe fussing all over them. Clive could hardly contain himself.

'I'll go over and take her spoon away,' he said.

'Clive,' I said. 'She hasn't used it yet.'

'I'll go over and wipe her forehead then,' he said. 'Maybe dab at her a bit with a napkin.'

'Clive,' I said. 'Stay where you are. Look – Dad!'

He had come into the restaurant, probably to see that Daphne Spurter was OK. Clive and I turned our backs to him and kept out of sight. When we turned back again, he had gone.

'Phew,' Clive said. 'That was close.'

It had been too. We didn't want Dad to see us, any more than we wanted him to know that we (well, Clive) had nobbled two of Gilbert Rimsey's waiters.

'More champagne, waiter!' I heard Mr Swanker Watson call, as he upended empty bottle number two into the ice-bucket.

'Do you think you should, dear?' Mrs Swanker Watson said.

'Course we should!' Mr Swanker said. 'Twenty

years of marriage . . . twenty years . . . twenty long, long years . . . twenty long, long, long years – happy years too, of course, very happy years – but long, yes long, yes, twenty ecstatically happy, but long, long, long, long years . . . Let's have another bottle.'

'Hey! You two!'

It was Monsieur Philippe.

'Miss Spurter's table. They've finished the first course. Needs clearing.'

'Come on, Clive.'

Daphne Spurter's party was sitting at a large, rectangular table. Clive started clearing from one side, I took the other. Clive was like a man in a daze, not really knowing what he was doing. He took Daphne Spurter's plate away like it was a holy relic.

'I was *that* close to her,' he said to me later, as we wheeled our trolleys to the kitchen. '*That* close to a living legend. I think she liked me too, you know.'

'Why do you say that, Clive?'

'Because as I was clearing her dishes, she looked at my name badge and said, "Thank you, Paulo, and could you ask the food waiter to bring us another bread roll – and sharpish".'

'Bring us another bread roll – and sharpish? Are you sure she said that, Clive?'

'Well, something like that. I think I might ask her for her autograph. I think I might rip my shirt open and ask her to write her name in felt-tipped pen across my heart.'

'Not now, Clive. We have to be discreet, remember. She might think it a bit unusual if the waiter ripped his shirt open.'

What happened next all occurred so suddenly that it is now something of a blur, and while I don't want you to think that I'm picking on Clive in any way and am always trying to blame him for everything, I can't deny that he had a hand in it all.

You see, there were two doors to the kitchen. Both swing doors. One for going in, one for coming out. You could kick them open, even with your hands full; even if you had four or five plates balanced up your arms, you could still get through in one smooth, continuous motion.

The traffic to and from the kitchen was pretty heavy, and plainly there was an In door and an Out door so as to keep things moving and to avoid any collisions.

Clive got distracted. I think it was Daphne Spurter who did it. Clive was so besotted with her that instead of looking where he was going, he was looking to where he had come from, and as a result was pushing his bus towards the Out door instead of the In.

He was about three metres from the door itself when a waiter flew out, carrying two trays with four plates on each tray, the whole arrangement balanced by years of experience.

He saw Clive. He saw Clive's trolley. He saw that if

he didn't do something, a collision was inevitable. So he swerved to the left to avoid Clive; Clive swerved the same way to avoid him; the waiter swerved the other way, picking up speed as he went, the trays with the plates of food on them seeming to take on a momentum of their own.

He darted past Clive. The plates and trays appeared to be trying to get away from him now, and he looked to be chasing after them. The faster they went, the faster he had to go, to stop them from falling.

So there they were – the trays chasing the plates and the waiter chasing the trays – the whole lot bearing down with increasing speed towards a table in the corner at which sat a quiet couple, enjoying their twentieth anniversary celebrations.

'Here's to us . . .' were the last words I heard, and I seem to recollect seeing somebody raising a champagne glass.

And then there was the loud crash, which seemed to go on for about six minutes. And then there was a silence. And then there was a figure, which seemed in some ways to bear a faint resemblance to Mr Swanker Watson – though in other ways it also bore a striking resemblance to a large heap of spaghetti covered in lamb chops, a roast duck, two vegetarian specials, a Dover sole and a lobster.

I looked at Clive, and Clive looked at me.

'You know,' Clive said. 'We've been working here

'nearly two hours now, and we've not had a break.'

'You're right, Clive,' I nodded. 'We've not.'

'Now might be a good time to take one,' Clive said.

'It might, Clive,' I agreed. 'It might be just the moment.'

'How about we nip out here,' Clive said, 'out by the service entrance? Before anyone sees us going. Like Gilbert Rimsey, for example.'

'Excellent thinking, Clive,' I said. 'A short break would do us no end of good.'

'In fact,' Clive said. 'There might be no call for us to come back.'

'You're right, Clive,' I said. 'I'm sure they'll manage without us now. We've done the heavy stuff. It'll be easy going for them from now on.'

'Shall we then . . . ?' Clive said, heading for the service door.

'Right.'

We got the door open just as Gilbert Rimsey came out from the kitchen. He saw eight of his gourmet dinners piled up on top of Mr Swanker Watson.

'What the ****'s going on here?' he said. 'What are you doing wearing eight ******* dinners on your head? This is a restaurant, not a ******* hat shop! I hope you're going to ******* pay for them!'

And then I heard Mr Swanker Watson's voice, faintly calling from behind the spaghetti for the wine waiter.

Clive and I made our way along the service corridor. Who should we run into than Paulo and Antonio, coming the other way.

'Hey, boys,' Antonio said. 'We feel a lot better now. We'll-a go back to work.'

'I wouldn't,' Clive warned. 'There's been an incident.'

But they insisted. So we gave them their jackets and name badges back, and Clive and me made ourselves scarce.

We went up to our penthouse suite and hid there, convinced that any moment Gilbert Rimsey would come haring up the fire escape, wielding a cleaver.

But he never did.

He didn't tell Dad about it either. Or perhaps he just never had the time. Because the next day something worse happened, something far worse than anything we could ever have imagined. And our days of penthouse luxury and our lives of privilege and pampering were suddenly over and at an end, and Clive and me were all alone in a hostile world, without a mum, without a dad, without anyone – without even so much as a roof to cover our heads.

11

The Safe

Dad worked such long hours, and we saw so little of him, that he might as well still have been a steward away at sea. In fact big ships and grand hotels have a lot in common, only one moves, and the other doesn't. But when it comes to managing them and keeping everybody in them happy, the pressures and demands are about the same.

Dad didn't usually get to bed until long after Clive and I had fallen asleep, and by the time we woke up, he was already dressed and on his way down to his office.

He kept in touch with Mrs Dominics on the phone every day or two, as she liked to get reports on how things were going, and whether there were any problems. She was only interested in really big problems though; dealing with little, minor, everyday problems was all part of Dad's duties and responsibilities.

Mrs Dominics seemed to move around a lot. One day she might be in the country in her mansion, the next she could be at one of her many other properties, making sure things were all up to scratch.

The following morning, there was a complaint waiting for Dad.

Clive and me were hanging around the front desk, waiting for Swanker to turn up so that we could do further explorations of London. We were planning on going on a boat trip up the Thames this time and then visiting the Tower of London, where lots of people had got their heads chopped off in the past. Clive said that when people got their heads chopped off, they dropped into a basket by the chopping block, and that if we were lucky, a few heads might still be in there and we would be able to see them, or possibly even pick them up by their ears and get our photos taken.

Clive also said that in the Tower of London there were blokes called Beefeaters, who were a bit like the pigeons in Trafalgar Square, only they preferred beef rather than birdseed. He said we should take some salami with us to feed them with.

While we were waiting, Mr Swanker Watson appeared at the reception desk and demanded to see the manager. To emphasize the point – and the urgency of the matter – he thumped the counter with his fist a couple of times, and then let out a loud yell, as he had accidentally banged his hand on a pen holder and skinned his knuckles.

Dad came out from his office and asked Mr Swanker Watson what he could do to help him.

'I was assaulted by one of your waiters last night,' Mr Swanker said. 'He dumped half a dozen dinners, including spaghetti and meatballs, all over me. It completely ruined our anniversary dinner, and I want to know what you're going to do about it. And while I'm here, I don't know if you know this, but you seem to have some underage illegal immigrants working in your Grill restaurant as dish collectors.'

'Oh?' Dad said. 'That's news to me.'

'Two smarmy-looking little hooligans,' Mr Swanker said. 'From the back streets of Naples, I wouldn't be surprised. No bigger than these two,' he said, spotting Clive and me loitering near the pillar. 'Only with a lot more hair-gel. It looked like child-exploitation to me. They plainly weren't up to the job either. One of them seemed a bit backward and slow on the uptake . . .'

'That'll be you, Clive,' I whispered.

'. . . while the other one seemed to have had his brains removed completely.'

'That'll be you then,' Clive said. (Which I thought was unnecessary and very rude.)

'I didn't get their names exactly,' Mr Swanker

went on, 'as my vision was obscured by all the spaghetti that landed on my head. But they definitely had name badges on. I think one of them might have been called Dumbo and the other one was called Tweetie Pie, or something, only more foreign and Italian-sounding, maybe like Dumbo-rini and Tweetie Pie-onardo or something like that. And what's more, that spaghetti sauce went all down the back of my collar and completely ruined my suit. So what are you going to do about it?'

Dad – uncharacteristically – seemed momentarily at a loss. His glance fell on me and Clive, as if he half suspected that we might have had something to do with it all. But then he must have realized that such suspicions were unfounded and such thoughts were unworthy of him, and he looked back at Mr Swanker.

'Mr Watson,' Dad said. 'This is the first I've heard of this. I'm afraid I knew nothing about it, and I can't tell you how sorry I am.'

Mr Swanker looked happier already. It's amazing the effect a hands-up apology can have on people.

'I'm very sorry that your evening was ruined. Please allow the hotel to make it up to you by inviting you to have a free meal in any of our restaurants, along with a complimentary bottle of champagne.'

'Make it two bottles,' Mr Swanker said. 'Though my wife is very unhappy about this. Our anniversary was ruined. She's still up in bed sobbing. That's fourteen hours she's been sobbing now. I had to sleep in my earplugs.'

'Of course,' Dad said. 'I can understand that she would be upset. So, in addition to the meal . . .' He glanced down at something out of sight under the desk. He reached for it and put it on the reception counter in front of Mr Swanker. 'Do you know what this is, Mr Watson?' he asked.

Mr Swanker Watson studied it.

'I do, as a matter of fact,' he said. 'For I'm a man of business and affairs. I have seen such things before on many occasions in the course of my career. It is an envelope.'

'And inside,' Dad said, 'are two tickets for the premiere tonight of *Never Eat A Green Banana* at the Leicester Square cinema, starring Daphne Spurter, who, as you may know, is staying with us here at the hotel. She kindly gave me two tickets for tonight's premiere. I had hoped to use them myself. But if you and Mrs Watson would care to go, I'd be delighted for you to have them.'

Well, you could have knocked Mr Swanker Watson down with a feather – probably with half a feather, probably with no feather at all, probably just with the picture of a feather.

'Tickets?' he said. 'For the premiere? Oh my. If you knew how much my wife—'

'Please,' Dad said. 'You have them.'

147

'Well, thank you,' Mr Swanker said. 'Thank you very, very much indeed. And please forget all about that other thing – the spaghetti and so on.'

He took the premiere tickets out of the envelope and looked at them in awe.

'The A-list?!' he said. 'You mean this will admit us to the private party afterwards too?'

'Of course,' Dad said.

'Hobnobbing with celebrities, behind the cordoned-off section with the red carpet and the maroon velvet ropes?'

'That's the one,' Dad smiled, probably thinking how little it took to make some people happy.

'My wife . . .' Mr Swanker said. 'My wife . . . this . . . if you only knew . . . thank you, thank you very much indeed.'

And he hurried away towards the lift, anxious to tell Mrs Swanker the good news, just as it opened and Swanker came out.

He even paused to give Swanker a pat on the head.

'How are you, Horace?' he said. 'There's a good boy. Off around London with your friends, are you? Have a few pounds spending money, won't you? Treat your friends to lunch and ice-cream and a bottle of pop.'

'Make it two bottles,' Clive called. And Mr Watson actually gave Swanker another fiver. Then he went off in the lift.

'I don't think I've ever seen my dad so cheerful,' Swanker said. 'What's got into him?'

'Search me,' I said. 'But never mind that, let's get going to the Tower of London. Clive wants to get his photograph taken with someone's head from the chopping basket. Bye, Dad!' I called.

'Bye, you two,' he said. 'Be back by five, won't you? And when you get back, I'd like a word with you about a few things – OK?'

He gave us one of his looks – the sort of look that seems to see right inside you, as if he knew all about everything and precisely what had been going on.

'Eh, sure, Dad,' I said.

'Right you are, Dad,' Clive nodded.

Then before he could say anything else, we were off, the three of us, out into the busy London street, and heading towards the river.

But Dad never did have that word with us.

The opportunity never came.

It was nearer six o'clock than five when Clive, Swanker and I got back to the Hotel Royal. We'd had a long, tiring and enjoyable day, only slightly marred by Clive's disappointment at not finding any heads in a basket round at the Tower of London. He had also not had much success in trying to feed salami to one of the Beefeaters, but that aside, things had gone swimmingly.

The hotel lobby was as busy as ever, with plenty of

coming and going. Some photographers and TV crews were already lurking outside, waiting for Daphne Spurter to appear and to climb into her car to drive to Leicester Square. (Though she could have walked it in a couple of minutes.) The film was due to begin at eight o'clock, with celebrities and guests arriving from seven onwards.

Swanker said cheerio to us and went up to his room. Clive and I were considering what to do next – whether we should have an ice-cream sundae in the Hot Muffin Café, or pie and chips in the Tearooms – when Mrs Swanker Watson flounced down the stairs, all dressed up in her going-to-a-premiere gear. She went to the reception desk, elbowed her way to the front and said, 'Manager, please,' to the clerk.

Dad must have heard her from his office, as he came straight out.

'Mrs Watson,' he said. 'How nice.' (He didn't say what was nice, but she plainly thought he meant her.)

'Mr Johnson,' she said, 'my jewellery from the safe, if you please.'

'Of course, Mrs Watson. Come through, if you would.'

Mrs Swanker headed for the office, and as she did, Daphne Spurter appeared, every inch the film star, also dressed in her going-to-a-premiere gear – only there was a lot less of it than Mrs Swanker had on, and she had a lot more to fill it with.

Clive went all swoony again.

'I'm in love,' he said. 'If it gets any worse, I'll have to breathe into a paper bag.'

'Pull yourself together, Clive,' I said. 'It's not love at all. It's just infatuation. You know that you and Daphne Spurter can never be. For a start she's about two feet taller than you in her high heels; on top of that she's a Hollywood film star worth millions, and you're a spotty oik with about fifty-six pence to his name; and then there's the age difference.'

'Age doesn't matter,' Clive said. 'When she's ninety-six, I'll be eighty-one. The difference won't matter at all then. We'll be as old as each other.'

I was impressed that Clive had worked these figures out on his own without a calculator, as he is normally not good at sums.

'And then when she's a hundred and fifteen,' he continued, 'I'll be forty-nine . . .' And I realized he'd just got lucky.

'You should set your sights on someone nearer your own age and circumstances, Clive,' I said. 'How about that girl we see at the bus stop in the mornings? The one in the football shirt with the nose ring, the tongue stud, the tattoo of the skull-and-crossbones, and the personal hygiene problem? I'm sure that once you get to know her she's a very nice person indeed. And you could always buy her some soap.'

But he wasn't listening. He was just standing there

panting, like an Old English Sheepdog left out in the garden on a hot summer's day.

I was quite surprised really. I'd never realized before that Clive had such a long tongue. But then I suppose that years of licking plates clean had probably done that.

'Oh, Mr Johnson,' Daphne Spurter drawled, in her laid-back American accent. She did have a certain something, I had to admit. When she spoke, it made your toes tingle. 'Could I get my necklace from the safe, please?'

'Of course, Miss Spurter,' Dad said. 'Please come into the office. I was just about to open the safe for this lady.' And Dad gestured to one of the hotel security guards to keep an eye out for any jewel thieves.

I don't think that Mrs Swanker Watson was all that pleased to see Daphne Spurter. That is, she was probably pleased to see her and to stand so close to her and to now be able to tell everyone when she got home that, 'I was as close to Daphne Spurter as I am to you right now. And let me tell you, she isn't up to much.' Only Daphne Spurter *was* up to much. She was up to so much that she left Mrs Swanker quite in the shade. I didn't think that Mrs Swanker liked the shade. Not when she was the one in it.

'Errol ...' Dad called. He nodded for the security man to come over and stand guard by the office door.

'I'll just open the safe now,' Dad said, and he closed the door on himself, Mrs Swanker and Daphne Spurter.

'Cor, imagine that,' Clive said. 'Imagine being in a room with the door closed with Daphne Spurter. Dad has all the luck.'

'Imagine being in a room with the door closed with Mrs Swanker though, Clive,' I said.

He started hyperventilating again then, and I had to slap him on the back for a while and then give him the Stroganov Manoeuvre, which is a medical procedure designed to stop people from fainting, in which you get them round the neck and twist their noses hard. It is best not to try this at home though, not unless you have had training.

'Come on, Clive,' I said, when he could breathe properly again. 'Let's go and get that ice-cream sundae. We can sign it to the room.'

'OK,' Clive said. 'Whose room shall we sign it to this time?'

But before I could answer him there was a scream. It was the longest, loudest scream I had ever heard. It seemed to go on and on and on. It sounded as if someone were having a baby – well, several babies, all at once.

And the screams were coming from Dad's office.

'Clive . . . ?' I said.

'What is it?' he said.

'It sounds like – Mrs Swanker!'

'You don't – you don't think Dad's . . . murdered her?' Clive said.

'No. Surely not. That would be Mr Swanker's job. Dad's not got the motivation.'

Another piercing scream came from the office.

'I know,' I said. 'Maybe she's suddenly found out somehow that the dress she's wearing is available elsewhere at half the price, or maybe—'

But then the door to the manager's office was thrown open, and there inside we saw an hysterical Mrs Swanker, a Daphne Spurter who had gone pale as snow beneath her California suntan, and Dad, looking ashen and shocked.

Behind him the door to the safe was open.

And the safe was completely empty.

'My jewellery!' Mrs Swanker Watson shrieked. 'My priceless jewellery! It's gone! It was worth thousands.'

'And mine, honey,' Daphne Spurter told her. 'And that cost eight million bucks! Five million pounds in your money!'

'But that's impossible,' we heard Dad say. 'Utterly impossible. I put the jewellery into the safe myself. And nobody else knows the combination – just me. Nobody else could have opened it.'

The two women turned, and they gave Dad such a look – such an accusing, distrustful, suspicious look.

Daphne Spurter turned to the security guard.

'Call the cops,' she said.

Dad looked as if the ground had vanished from under him. He looked completely and utterly shocked.

'Clive,' I said. 'We're in deep trouble here.'

'Big time,' he agreed. 'Big time.'

'Clive,' I said. 'They think Dad did it. It's down to us to clear his name.'

'We'll do it,' he said. 'We'll do it – won't we?'

We stood there, each as shocked as the other. A silence moved through the lobby, like an elephant passing by.

And then we heard the sirens out in the street.

12

Arrest

It all happened so fast that had it happened any faster, it probably wouldn't have happened at all.

The hotel lobby was suddenly full of policemen and photographers, with the policemen trying to get the photographers to go back outside onto the street. One of the young officers was saying, 'I don't believe it, it's Daphne Spurter! Wait till I get her autograph!' while Mrs Swanker Watson was having hysterics.

Mr Swanker Watson appeared from the lift and demanded to know what was going on, but the only words he could get out of Mrs Swanker were: 'My gems, my gems, my precious gems!' before she collapsed into hysterics again, demanding that Mr Swanker do something about it, but not telling him what *it* was.

Mr Swanker started to bang his head softly against

a pillar, moaning 'Not again, not again,' to himself and saying it was enough to drive a man to drink, whereupon a waiter with a tray – who must have overheard him – asked if he could get Mr Swanker anything, and Mr Swanker said yes, a large whisky. A large bottle, that was, and the waiter needn't bother with a glass.

While all this was going on, Daphne Spurter's hangers-on and her full entourage of personal assistant, hairdresser, personal assistant's personal assistant, her personal astrologer, her personal bodyguard (whose job it was to stop strangers from getting too personal), her friend from home who had known her personally since they'd been at school together (only the friend wasn't so pretty), her personal manicurist, her personal publicist, her personal adviser, her personal financial adviser, her personal dietician, her personal dog-walker, her personal dog Timbles (in person), her personal trainer, her personal spiritual guru and her personal relationships counsellor, along with other various person or persons unknown, were all milling around her talking, shouting, gesticulating and screeching at once, saying things like, 'My gawd, Daphne, honey!' (For they were mostly Americans.) And 'Shucks, Daphne!' And 'Your jewels, Daphne! Where are they?' And 'Who's the bum who stole them?' ('Bum' is also an American expression. It does not mean the same as when it applies to Clive.

A 'bum' in American is a down-and-out. In Clive's case a bum is the fat thing opposite his head that he spends most of his life sitting on.)

It was complete chaos and Dad seemed to be at the centre of it, doing his best to calm things down and to protest his innocence in the face of a rising tide of accusations – all false too, as Clive and I knew. We knew our dad hadn't taken the jewellery – but we were quite unable to prove it, or even get anyone to listen to us.

Clive and I got pushed away to the edge of the commotion, and though we tried to worm our way back towards the centre, we kept getting shoved aside.

'That's my dad!' Clive was shouting. 'You leave him alone!' But his voice was eclipsed by the voices of others, especially that of Mrs Swanker Watson, demanding that the police do something immediately, like get her jewellery back, as if she expected one of the policemen to find it in his helmet.

'*He* was the last to see it! *He* put it in the safe! *He's* the only one who knows the combination! It must be him!'

'But – if you'd just please listen – just a moment, please . . .'

Only nobody *was* listening, not to Dad, not to Clive, and not to me. They all seemed swept up in the madness of it all. I think it was the fact that

Daphne Spurter, a real live Hollywood film star, was standing there which made them all act so irrationally. They were overexcited, anxious that something be done, right here, right now.

'Daphne, honey,' one of her entourage said. 'With or without the necklace, we're gonna have to go to this premiere . . .'

Which set Mrs Swanker Watson off again.

'The premiere!' she wailed. 'I'm going to miss the premiere! I was going to wear my diamonds to it. I could all but see the light of the flashbulbs glinting off them. And now all I've got to wear around my neck is nothing!'

'I can lend you a piece of string!' I heard Clive shouting. 'If you leave our dad alone!'

But nobody heard him apart from me. Or if they did, they paid no attention. The waiter had arrived with Mr Swanker Watson's whisky now, and he was pouring himself a large one.

'Always the same,' he was saying. 'Always the same. You're better off staying at home.'

And he downed his large one in a gulp.

The next thing I heard were fragments of what one of the policemen was saying to Dad. His words were broken up by all the noise and commotion around him.

'Have to ask you . . .' he was saying. 'Accompany us . . . station . . . cooperate . . . serious allegations . . . until such time . . . charges . . .'

I saw Dad frantically looking around the crowd – probably looking for us, for me and Clive – and I heard him say something like, 'No – my two boys – not without them . . .'

Then I heard the words which sent the deep chills right into me.

'. . . not to worry about them,' the policeman said. Then the next bit was garbled: '. . . something . . . something . . . something.' Then I heard the awful words, '. . . look after them . . . get someone . . . care for them . . .'

I heard Dad calling out for us, and we called back to him and we tried to force our way through the crush. But by the time we had got to the door, Dad had gone, and a police car was driving away, with him in the back of it. He looked back as the car turned the corner. I don't know if he saw us or if he didn't, but he looked as pale as death.

'Clive,' I said. 'I don't believe it – a moment ago everything was fine, and now . . .'

We didn't know where to turn, so we turned back, into the hotel lobby. The crowd was thinning out now and people were calming down. Daphne Spurter was being ushered out to a waiting limousine. Jewels or no jewels, she had to go to her premiere. Mrs Swanker Watson was drying her eyes and pulling herself together. It was the same with her. She too had a premiere to attend, and she wasn't going to miss the chance to do some serious swanking.

'Come along, Charles,' she said to Mr Swanker. 'Let us go get a cab and make our way to the premiere. We may not have our jewels, but we still have our dignity.'

'Yush, dear,' Mr Swanker said – who did not seem to have quite as much dignity as he'd had five minutes ago, before he'd unscrewed the top off a whisky bottle.

They headed for the door, either ignoring us completely or not seeing us at all.

I stared at Clive. He was looking more worried than I'd ever seen him.

'Did you hear what they said?' he kept saying. 'Did you hear what that policeman said?'

'Huh, Clive? What do you mean?'

'Care,' he said. 'They're going to take us into Care . . .'

'No,' I said. 'He didn't say that. He said "take care", didn't he?'

'No,' Clive said. 'We've got to get out of here. Quick. Before anyone comes for us. They've got Dad, and they're coming back for us. To take us into Care. But they can't do that, because we've got to prove that Dad's innocent. And how can we do that, if we've been taken into Care?'

I didn't know. I thought Clive had heard wrong. I thought the policeman had said 'take care' not 'take into Care'. But I wasn't sure. And, of course, Clive was right. We had to prove that Dad was innocent. It was down to us. We knew he was, of course we did – our dad was so straight and honest that he could have gone and been a monk (only I didn't know if monks were allowed to have ladies stay overnight in their cells as they are too tired to go home, which is a sort of charity work that Dad used to do from time to time, as well as lending the ladies one of his old shirts to wear in the morning when they came down for breakfast).

I just wasn't sure, that was all, about what had been said. But I knew we couldn't afford to risk it.

'They're coming,' Clive said. 'Look!'

Sure enough, two policemen and a policewoman were entering by the revolving door. They went up to the desk and said, 'We're looking for Mr Johnson's two boys . . .'

'Go, Clive!' I hissed. 'Go!'

And we were off.

'They were here just a minute ago,' I heard the receptionist say. 'They were standing right . . . oh. They seem to have gone. But they must be in the hotel somewhere. They can't be far away.'

'Right,' the policeman said. 'We'd better go find them. Which room are they staying in?'

I didn't hear any more. We were out of the lobby and down the corridor, the one which led towards the rear of the hotel. We rounded a corner and paused a moment.

'Which way?' Clive said.

'The room,' I said. 'The penthouse suite.'

'But they'll look there.'

'I know they will, Clive,' I said. 'But all our things are there. We can't just run away with nothing. We can't go and live on the streets of London with nothing but the clothes we stand up in. We've got to get there before they do, chuck a few things in a bag, grab some supplies from the fridge, find what money we can, and go.'

'But . . . but . . . how's that going to help Dad?'

'I dunno, Clive. But first things first. So come on. Let's go.'

We ran the length of the corridor until we came to the lift. We got in, punched the button, and zoomed up to the penthouse.

'What do we need?' Clive said. 'What'll we take with us? What should I take?'

'As much as possible and as little as you can!' I said, grabbing my duffle bag and stuffing things into it.

'Eh?' Clive said. 'What does that mean?'

'Just take the bare necessities, Clive,' I said.

He began to unplug the wide-screen television.

'No, Clive!' I said. 'The necessities for living out on the street – if we have to. Warm clothes. Toothbrush. Stuff like that. Keep it to one bag.'

We filled a bag each with what we needed. We took all the snacks and peanuts from the fridge, along with some bottles of water.

Then we heard a noise, a clank and a drone.

'Listen,' Clive said. 'It's the lift.'

Someone down below had summoned it. It was on its way to them.

'Have you got everything, Clive?' I said.

'Think so, only—'

The lift had stopped, far down beneath us. The drone resumed. The lift was coming back up.

'They're coming for us,' Clive said. 'They're coming up. They'll be here any moment. What do we do?'

'Fire escape!' I said.

'No!' Clive said. 'Too obvious. First place they'll look. We'll never get to the bottom in time. They'll catch us. Or they'll radio for another policeman to be at the bottom.'

I could see that he was right.

The drone was growing louder, the lift was getting nearer. Clive was starting to squirm, like he does when he's desperate for the toilet.

'What do we do, what do we do, what do we do!'

Then I saw it.

'Balcony. Outside. Duck down. Stock-still. Now!'

The lift had arrived. I could hear it shuddering to a stop. Any second the door would open and the policemen would walk in and—

'Go!'

We were out on the balcony, the door softly closing behind us.

We lay down on the balcony floor, right under the window, so that even if somebody looked out, we couldn't be seen.

We held our breath, and waited.

I saw that Clive had his hands together, as if he were saying a prayer.

'No. No one in here.'

They spent a good twenty minutes looking. In some ways I think they were more interested in seeing what a penthouse suite in the Hotel Royal had to offer than in finding me and Clive in a hurry.

Clive had been right though, for a change. When they discovered that we weren't in the apartment, the first place they looked was . . .

'See if they legged it down the fire escape.'

I heard the door to the fire escape open; heard the rattle of heavy boots on metal. I even saw the police officer, there on the top platform of the escape. Had he turned round, he would have seen us.

He was peering down below him, down to the side alleyway, with its cardboard boxes where the rough sleepers spent their homeless evenings, in the shadow of this great hotel – where a single night in the cheapest room cost more money than they could beg or borrow in a month, and where a week in the penthouse would have cost thousands.

'No. Not there. Didn't go out that way. Maybe they didn't come up here at all.'

I willed him to go back inside. But he didn't. He stayed there on the platform of the fire escape, looking down, enjoying the vertigo and the view of the rooftops and the satellite dishes.

They're funny things rooftops, you so rarely see them. They're a bit ragged and untidy, most of them, with things stuck on the top of them – heating boilers and air-conditioning units – some even have little gardens, some actually have swimming pools. Some have huge gardens. I even spotted one in London with real trees on the roof.

The backs of buildings were funny too. Especially such grand places like the Hotel Royal. From the front they're all swank and splendour. But at the back, they're all drainpipes and wheelie bins and cats with their heads in the rubbish.

'Go away,' I willed the policeman. 'Go back inside!'

I looked at Clive to see if he was all right. He was there next to me on the balcony, where we were lying face to face.

At first I thought he was having some kind of fit, as he was making these horrible grimaces. But then I realized that it was worse than that.

He was going to sneeze. A hair must have tickled him, or maybe it was due to the light, which seems to make you sneeze sometimes, especially if you glance at the sun.

I could see it coming. It was as inevitable as

tomorrow. The sneeze. The noise. The policeman turning round. Him seeing us. Us getting dragged off. No one to prove Dad's innocence. Dad sent to prison. Us taken into Care – or sent to live for ever with Grandma and Granddad and his big corduroy trousers.

So I did what I had to.

For people of a sensitive disposition, it might be best to skip the next few lines and to press on elsewhere. But for those who prefer reality and who can stomach the facts, no matter how unpleasant they are, well, the facts are these.

I had to do something to stop Clive sneezing.

So I did what I had to do.

I did it without any thought for myself, for my own safety, for the sacrifice I was making, or for the possibly fatal consequences it might have for my long-term mental and physical well-being.

I did what I did for the greater good. And I want you to remember that. I mean, I'm not saying what I did was beyond the normal run of heroism, and I'm not asking for medals or expecting mentions in dispatches or anything like that. All I'm saying is that sometimes a brother has to do what a brother has to do.

And so I did it.

I stuck a finger up each of Clive's nostrils.

He gave me a most peculiar look. His eyes seemed like two question marks. What are you doing? they seemed to say. That's my job. That's my hobby. Not yours.

But he didn't sneeze.

A few moments later the policeman went back inside. I found a tissue in my pocket.

I expected Clive to erupt with indignation and go on at me for what I'd done. But he didn't. He just stared at me, from a few inches away, and he spoke in a whisper.

'Do it again,' he said.

But there was no way I was doing a thing like that twice in a lifetime.

I still shudder now when I think about it, and some nights I can't sleep at all, what with the memories and the flashbacks. I think it's called Post-Traumatic Stress Syndrome. When I get older I shall probably have to have therapy. Sometimes I get these dreams in which I go into the kitchen, find a cleaver, and chop two of my fingers off. Fortunately it hasn't actually come to that yet. I just hope I don't start walking in my sleep.

We heard the faint drone of the lift from within the penthouse.

'They've gone,' I said.

We got stiffly to our feet and went back inside.

What now? I wondered. Where now?

Clive seemed to read my thoughts.

'We may as well stay here then,' he said. 'They won't be coming back.'

'No,' I said. 'We can't risk it. The maid'll come in. They'll give the suite to somebody else. They're not going to let it stand empty. They might even move Daphne Spurter in here.'

'Where then?' Clive said. 'Where do we go? I mean, it's starting to get dark.'

It was too. The sun had turned purple and was sinking down behind the rooftops. I bet not many people know this, but there are three different kinds of twilight. We did it once at school. There's Civil Twilight, Nautical Twilight, and Astronomical Twilight. In a way, they're all different degrees of darkness, and Astronomical Twilight is the darkest of all. That is when the sun has sunk completely down below the horizon, and not even a remnant of its afterglow can be seen.

That was the twilight we waited for, and then we slipped out to the fire escape, carrying our few possessions, and we said goodbye to the high life, to our penthouse suite and our luxury-living. We walked silently down the metal fire escape, like condemned men walking to their execution.

We were all alone in the world again, me and Clive, just like we seemed to be sometimes. Sometimes you feel ever so alone. It was bad enough not to have our mum, but now we didn't have our dad either. He'd been taken away and accused of terrible crimes that he hadn't done, and it was down to me and Clive to save him – but in all honesty, I didn't know how.

I felt so lonely, but I didn't say so as I wanted to keep morale up, and so I tried to hum a happy tune and seem cheerful.

'You know something,' Clive said, as we walked on down the fire escape, keeping low when we passed any windows, in case someone looked out and saw us.

'What's that, Clive?' I said.

'I feel ever so lonely,' he said. 'And a bit frightened.'

But that's Clive for you. No shame. Always wearing his heart on his sleeve. No thoughts for morale.

'Me too, Clive,' I said. 'Me too.'

He stopped a while and we looked at the stars.

'I'm glad you're here,' he said.

And I almost told him I was glad that he was there too.

But in the end, I thought better of it.

13

This Way Up

'What now? What are we going to do?'

Good question.

We were at the bottom of the fire escape, down in the alley at the side of the Hotel Royal.

It was like being a couple of fish in the ocean, two small sardines, hiding in a crevice, while the great tides and billows of the immense, raging sea, ebbed and flowed around us. If we stayed where we were though, we were safe – for a while.

London was out there, just down at the end of the alley and turn left. Or right. Or walk straight on. And there it all was, the colossal, endless city, full of ceaseless bumper-to-bumper traffic, roaring buses and squealing taxis, full of shops that never closed and people who never seemed to go to bed, or who had no beds to go to. It was full of noise and crowds and other alleyways, and streets, and endless houses, and millions and millions of people, not one of whom we knew, or knew us, or who would help us.

'I want to go home,' Clive said.

Only where was home from here? How did you get there? And how could we go to it anyway, when Dad was in trouble, and we had to make it right? We couldn't desert him. We were his only chance. He'd never let us down when we had problems, so we had to do the same for him now.

'First,' I said, 'we have to find somewhere to sleep. Then we have to make a plan.'

'What about eating?' Clive said. 'When do we do that?'

'When don't you?' I said, in a sarcastic tone, just to let him know who was the eldest.

'We can't go to bed with no tea,' Clive said.

'Eat your peanuts that you took from the fridge.'

'I already have. I ate them on the way down the fire escape.'

'All right. Let's see. How much money have you got?'

We counted out what we had. It wasn't much, but it was enough to keep us going.

'OK,' I said. 'Let's walk down to Piccadilly and get some pizza slices and some drinks.'

Which is what we did.

We took our slices to Leicester Square and sat on a bench to eat them. The people just never stopped.

It was like they were coming out of the ground somewhere. Which some of them were, as they'd travelled there on the Underground.

'What are they all doing here?' Clive said. 'Where are they all coming from?'

I didn't know, but on they came.

'Look,' I said. 'Over there.'

There was a cluster of people waiting outside the cinema with pens and autograph books. On a hoarding mounted on the cinema frontage was a huge photograph of Daphne Spurter and the name of her film: *Never Eat A Green Banana*. Alongside it were some quotes from favourable film reviews. *Never seen anything like it before!* one of them said. I guessed that the rest of it – which had been omitted – probably said something along the lines of: *And I never want to either!* But perhaps I was being cynical.

Premiere here tonight! the lettering above the cinema entrance read, and the red carpet was still in place, and half a dozen security guards in evening jackets were standing in a line – maybe to make sure that nobody left the film before it had finished.

'What are we going to do?' Clive asked again.

'Do you have to keep saying that, Clive?' I said. 'You're a bit too much on the one note, you know.'

'Yeah, but what are we going to do?'

'We'll have to make a plan.'

Clive chewed on his pizza.

'How are we going to make a plan?' he said.

'Questions, questions, Clive,' I said. 'With you it's always questions, questions.'

'Is it?' he said.

'There you go again,' I told him.

'But what are we going to do? Where are we going to stay tonight? How are we going to prove that Dad didn't take the diamonds from the safe?'

'I'm working on it,' I said. 'One thing at a time.'

As I chewed on my pizza, I noticed a wheelie bin next to a building in a corner of the square.

In London the rubbish trucks don't just turn up in the morning, often they work all through the night, taking all the garbage away. Fortunately they hadn't been round yet.

'Clive,' I said. 'That's where we sleep.'

He followed my gaze.

'What?' he said. 'In a dustbin?'

'Like it would be the first time for you, I suppose, Clive,' I said, as he was starting to get on my nerves a bit with his negative attitudes and the way he always pours scorn on my constructive suggestions. 'I mean, let's face it, you all but wear a dustbin, in fact, dustbins follow you down the road.'

'I'm not sleeping in a dustbin,' Clive said, in his stubborn voice. 'There might have been cabbage in it. Some of us have standards, you know.'

'No, I don't mean the dustbin. I mean next to the bins. The boxes. We get ourselves a couple of those

176

big cardboard boxes, we take them back to the alleyway by the Hotel Royal, and we sleep there.'

'What? In Cardboard City?'

'Well, Cardboard Alley, yeah.'

'With the down-and-outs?'

'Clive,' I reminded him. 'We *are* down and out.'

'I can't believe it,' Clive said. 'Yesterday my life was a beautiful painting. It looked wonderful from all angles. There I was, living on the knee of luxury—'

'Lap of luxury,' I corrected him.

'Whatever. And now, just twenty-six hours later—'

'Twenty-four, Clive. There's twenty-four hours in a day.'

'Not in leap years,' he said, and I was too fed up to argue with him. 'And now,' he said, 'we've gone from the penthouse suite to homeless, just like that.'

'Just like what?'

'Like that!'

Clive tried to snap his fingers, but his snap wouldn't work.

'Look, Clive,' I said. 'I'm tired and that's my best suggestion. If you've got a better one, I'm ready to listen to it.'

'OK,' he said. 'Let's get the boxes.'

So that was what we did.

I guess that in another town we would have looked suspicious – two small boys crossing a busy square carrying two large cardboard boxes, one marked

This way up (and you can guess which way up Clive was carrying it) and the other marked *Fragile* (which just about described the state of my nerves). But even the policemen patrolling the Square didn't pay us much attention.

There were eight million stories in the big city, and ours was just one of them. And by London standards, ours wasn't that strange at all, and two small boys with large boxes were not of much interest to anyone.

So we headed for the alleyway, to find ourselves a space where we could put our bits of cardboard down and get settled for the night.

Yes, we'd seen the high spots, had Clive and me, we'd tasted luxury and we'd known success, we'd mingled with swankers and rubbed shoulders with film stars, we'd eaten in gourmet restaurants and had had flunkeys at our beck and call, ready to do our bidding at the drop of a hat. (Not that we went in for that much. We don't do a lot of hat-dropping on the whole.) But now it was time for the other stuff, for the other side of the coin.

Yet I wasn't that downhearted. Because we'd known hardships before, had me and Clive, and no doubt we will know them again. We'd weathered the storm and picked up the challenge, and we'd come through smiling, so maybe our luck would change.

Once upon a time, we'd had to share

accommodation with various whiskery rodents down in rat class in the bowels of a ship. And now here we were on the skids again.

'You know what class we're in now, Clive, don't you?' I said, as we walked on back to the alley.

'What class is that then?' he said.

'Box class,' I told him. 'Cardboard box class.'

We came to the alleyway. It was dim and ill-lit after the neon glare of Piccadilly. It took your eyes a few moments to get used to it. I trod on, and then stumbled over something, as we made our way along, looking for a place to park our boxes.

'Oi!' a voice yelled from deep inside a box. I could just make out some lettering on it. It read: *Tinned Tomatoes*. 'Oi! Mind me feet!'

I didn't reply and hurried on. Our teacher at school, Miss Scrimshaw, had once warned us about talking to weirdos and strangers. I somehow suspected that talking to tinned tomatoes fell well within the scope of that warning.

There were about five or six cardboard boxes set out along the alleyway by the side of the Hotel Royal. It was obviously a sought-after and a popular area, being in the West End of London. It is important to have an up-market address when trying to make a mark for yourself in big cities, and this plainly applied to people in boxes as much as anyone else.

Clive and me found a spot towards the end of the

alleyway. It was on the dark and smelly side, but we felt that we couldn't be choosers, so Clive set out *This Way Up* and I placed *Fragile* next to it.

'Look,' Clive said, tilting back his head and looking upwards at the fire escape and the penthouse suite. 'That was us a short while ago. We didn't know how lucky we were. I wish I could have my bed back.'

'No sense in dwelling on it, Clive,' I said.

'Don't have a lot of choice, do I?' he said. 'I am dwelling on it. I'm flipping living in it – in a cardboard box, that used to belong to a washing machine or something, or a big computer.'

'Well, whatever it was, it was something that had to be *This Way Up*, Clive,' I said.

'Maybe it was an ostrich then,' he said.

'Don't be stupid. Ostriches don't come in cardboard boxes.'

'They have to be *This Way Up* though, don't they?'

'Well . . . maybe . . .'

'So I'm right then.'

There was no point in arguing with him, so I didn't. There is no sense in having debates with stupid people, as they are unable to understand the finer points.

'OK,' I said. 'We'd better get some sleep.'

Quite a lot of snoring was coming from the other boxes – so much in fact that I was worried it might keep us awake.

'Sounds like a chorus of bullfrogs,' Clive said. 'And I just thought of something – what do I do if I wake up and need the loo?'

Judging from the pong at the end of the alley, I would have thought that the answer to Clive's question was obvious.

'Just use your head, Clive,' I said.

'Eh?' he said. 'Use my head for what? How can I go to the loo with my head?'

'For working out where to go,' I said. I think he twigged on then, as he shut up.

We crawled into our boxes. I was curling up and trying to get comfortable in mine, when I heard a plaintive wail.

'Hello . . .'

It was Clive.

'I feel a bit lonely,' he said. 'I'm all on my own in here and I can't see anyone.'

I felt a bit on my own too, but I wasn't telling him that.

His head appeared around the front of my box.

'Can I punch a hole in your box?' Clive asked. 'Then, if I punch a hole in mine too, we'll be able to see each other.'

'How about I punch a hole in your head, Clive?' I said. 'And then you'll be able to see stars.'

'Go on,' he said. 'It'll be fun.'

So against my better judgement I let Clive go punching holes in the boxes so that as they lay

181

side by side we could see each other for a spot of reassurance.

I tried to get comfortable again, but became aware of a beady eyeball looking at me. It was him.

'Here,' Clive said. 'Your box is better than mine.'

'The other man's grass, Clive,' I said. 'The other man's grass.'

'What?' he said. 'Have you got a lawn in there then? That's not fair, if your box has got a lawn.'

'No, you idiot. The other man's grass is always greener. It's a saying. It means you think things are always better for other people, but they're not, they just seem to be. For grass, read boxes. The other man's box is always better.'

'Yours is nicer cardboard though,' Clive said.

'It's just the same as yours,' I said to the beady eyeball. 'There's no difference.'

'Yours is more comfy,' Clive said.

'For crying out— all right,' I said. 'Let's swap then! I don't care which box I have, I just want to get some sleep.'

So we crawled out of our boxes and swapped around. I curled up and tried to get comfortable again, when once again an eyeball appeared at the interconnecting holes.

'Hello . . .'

'What now, Clive?'

'I think maybe my box was better after all.'

'I'm going to kill you, Clive,' I said.

'Can I have it back?'

'No. I'm not moving again. Go to sleep.'

Clive started to make groaning and keening noises.

'Not fair,' he said. 'I want my box.'

He went on at such length about it that he woke all the other boxes up.

'For gawd's sake give him his box back,' a voice from the far end of the alley snapped. 'And let's all get some sleep. There's people here have to go to work in the morning.'

I was somewhat surprised to hear that.

'I've got a hard day's begging ahead of me,' the voice elaborated. 'Twelve hours of sitting out on a cold hard pavement, saying, "Hungry and homeless, spare some change". You need your beauty sleep for that sort of business.'

So, rather than cause trouble, I swapped round with Clive again and let him have *This Way Up* back. Again, I was just getting settled when the eyeball appeared at the hole.

'Hello . . .'

'No way, Clive,' I said.

'I just wanted to say goodnight.'

'Night, Clive.'

'If anyone comes round with any soup and I'm asleep at the time . . .'

'Yeah?'

'Get me some minestrone, with a bread roll and

some butter. White roll, that is, and unsalted butter if they've got it.'

'OK.'

'And some crunchy croutons.'

'Yes, Clive.'

'And a strawberry yoghurt for pudding.'

'Clive!!! Be quiet in there and close your eyes.'

At last he went to sleep.

14

A Night Out

I lay awake for a long time, wondering what to do and trying to work out a plan of action. Finally I slept too. But not for long, because the ground was hard and the night had grown cold. I couldn't help but think of penthouse suites and comfy beds and the life we had left behind. Then I thought of Dad, probably locked up on his own in a prison cell, and I worried about that too.

Dawn came early – too early for me. It woke me up, tired and shivering a little. I could hear coughing and snoring and sounds of movement coming from other boxes.

I peered through the hole to see what Clive was doing. He was lying there in his box, with his head on his arm, sleeping the sleep of the innocent – well, it was that or the sleep of the totally gormless.

It was all right for him, I thought. It was no worries for Clive. It was never any worries for people who don't know what worries are. But for me it was all worries. For I had to work out a plan for proving that Dad hadn't taken the diamonds, even though he had been the only one who had known the combination to the hotel safe.

But then, I thought, he couldn't have been the *only* one, because somebody else must have told him what the combination was in the first place. Only who?

And another thing, which proved to me that there had to be somebody else who knew the combination, was the risk involved. If the hotel manager was the only one who knew the combination, how was the safe to be opened if he forgot it? Just say he had an accident and lost his memory? Just say he had a heart attack and dropped down stone-dead? How was the safe to be opened then?

No, someone else had to know the combination. Only who?

Mrs Dominics, I guessed. Yes, that would make sense. Mrs Dominics would know, and she would have been the one who would have given the combination to Dad. So that meant that—

No. I couldn't believe that for an instant. Not Mrs Dominics. She wasn't going to open the safe in her own hotel and steal people's diamonds. She already had more diamonds than she knew what to do with. She had so many she could have gravelled her path with them. And anyway, she wasn't even there at the hotel. She'd left all that to Dad. She was at home in her stately mansion in the country probably, or even off visiting one of her other hotels, in Paris, or Rome, or Barcelona. She might even have gone off on another cruise, hoping to have adventures like she'd had with me and Clive, when we'd stowed away in rat class and had brightened up the trip no end.

So I lay in my box, pondering the unponderables, as the early-morning light crept in through the lid.

'Oi! *Fragile!*'

It was the voice which had told Clive and me off for making a racket last night.

'Oi! *Fragile!* I'm talking to you!'

I remembered that *Fragile* was me.

'Yus?' I said, in as deep and as growly a voice as I could manage.

'Soup and sandwiches is here,' the voice said. 'Tell your mate *This Way Up*. Don't dawdle, or you'll miss it.'

I could have done with some soup and sandwiches. It wasn't my usual breakfast, but it sounded all right to me.

Only . . .

But there's always an only when you're our age – me and Clive's age, that is. I was worried, you see, about us showing our faces. Because it's one thing to be grown up and homeless and living in a box, but to be nothing but a poor waif (although Clive is a bit fat for a waif) and living in a box is another thing. When people saw how old we were, they would instantly think that we weren't up to looking after ourselves. They'd happily leave grown-ups to live in cardboard boxes until the day they died, but children – well, no. They'd see that we were living rough and they'd . . .

Take us into Care. Which was what we'd run away from, which was why we were here. There was no way we were going to be able to help Dad if we were taken into Care.

And yet soup and sandwiches did sound nice. Piping-hot soup. Deep-filled, succulent sandwiches.

'Clive!'

He didn't wake.

'Clive!'

Nothing.

'Oi!'

I reached through the hole and gave him a flick on the ear.

'Gerroffame, whassup, worrayoudoing?'

'Clive,' I said. 'There's soup and sandwiches outside. It's the charity van for the homeless.'

'Lead me to it,' he said. 'Put a sarnie in either hand. Then set me loose and watch and wonder!'

He was already on his way out of his box.

'No, Clive!' I said. 'Wait. We can't let anyone know that we're just boys.'

'Why not?'

'They'll take us into Care, of course, if they see we're two boys sleeping rough.'

'Then – shall we pretend to be girls then? I can be Sybil and you can be Glenys, and I can talk with a lisp and you can walk with a waddle and show your bellybutton off.'

'No, Clive,' I said. 'For a start no one's going to believe you're a girl, not even if you put your hair in curlers and wear a party frock, and as for me, I'm far too manly to pass for anything less than Mr Universe.'

'Hmm, yes,' Clive said. 'I see what you mean. I suppose I could never really be mistaken for a girl either, not with muscles like mine.'

'Exactly, Clive,' I said. 'Most girls have far bigger muscles than you. But even if we were girls, we'd still get taken into Care anyway. It's our age that's the problem. Not that we're boys. And that's only part of the problem. In fact getting taken into Care is what'll happen if we're lucky.'

'And if we're unlucky?' Clive said, peering at me through the hole in the boxes.

'The white slave trade, Clive,' I said. 'Or, in your case, the slightly grubby-looking, grey slave trade.'

'The grey slave trade!' Clive said, his eyes widening in the dim light. 'What happens there?'

'It's when you get kidnapped,' I explained, 'and taken abroad. And you have to wear baggy pantaloons and special slippers with curly bits on the toes. And then you get put to work for some Arabian princess, and you have to give her baths in asp's milk and give her back rubs and make her cups of tea and scrub her down with a loofah.'

'Cor,' Clive said. 'Do you get paid much?'

'You don't get paid anything, you peanut brain. You're a slave.'

'Is she beautiful, the princess?' Clive said.

'I don't know. She might be.'

'Is she as beautiful as Daphne Spurter, the Hollywood actress and film star?'

'Possibly. She might be.'

'Oh. So where do you apply for the job then?' Clive asked.

'Clive,' I said, trying hard to keep my temper, for it annoys me sometimes the way Clive never seems to understand the point I'm making, almost as if he's doing so deliberately, 'Clive, being a slave isn't a job that you want to apply for. It's a horrible fate that befalls you.'

'Oh, I don't know,' he said. 'Scrubbing down beautiful princesses with a big sponge and giving them a bit of a hot wax and a polish after, it doesn't sound so bad to me. Not if you get your room and board as well. And do they let you have a PlayStation?'

'Clive!' I said, reaching through the hole to try and seize him by the throat, though he managed to elude my grasp. 'Listen to me for once, will you, and stop going off on tangents!'

'What's a tangent? Is it a sort of skateboard?'

'Never mind. Just listen. What we have to do, Clive, is act older than we are. Act older, act taller—'

'How do you—'

'Just listen. Act older, talk in deeper voices, and if anyone asks if we're kids, we say no. We tell them that we're forty-five, but we suffer from some kind of rare medical condition—'

'Like athlete's foot?'

'Some rare medical condition that has prevented us from growing to our full height and reaching our potential. And as a result we have been discriminated against and so have given in to depression and despair—'

'Story of my life,' Clive interjected. I ignored him.

'. . . depression and despair, and we've lost all our money, and our marriages have broken up—'

'Are we married then?' Clive said. 'I just thought we were brothers.'

'To other people! To girls!'

'And do they suffer from this disease as well?'

If I had been able to get through that hole, I would have killed Clive then. I would have torn both him and *This Way Up* into little pieces. As it was, I couldn't be bothered.

'Clive, forget everything I said. Leave the talking to me. Just remember – walk with a swagger, talk in a deep voice, and act as if you're forty-five. You ready?'

'Ready!'

'Let's go.'

'What do we do after?'

'You get back in your box.'

Clive clambered out of *This Way Up*, and I tentatively nosed my way out of *Fragile*. The pong at the end of the alley hadn't got any better. In fact I suspected that somebody had been topping it up during the night.

'Walk tall and act hard, Clive,' I said, and we made our way along the alley, walking tall and acting hard and talking in deep voices, going to join the other cardboard-box dwellers at the end of the lane, where a small van was parked. Two people were there, both with shaven heads and dressed in orange robes. One was ladling the soup out and one was handing out sandwiches.

'Got any spam sandwiches, mate?' one of the rough-sleepers asked. I noticed, to my surprise, that Clive and I were among the tallest there. We seemed to have chosen an alleyway of very short rough-sleepers. This was good, as it made us look older, by contrast, than we were.

'No spam, brother Barnsley,' the shaven-headed man with the sandwiches said. 'Vegetarian only.'

Brother Barnsley – as the man had called him – swore under his breath and settled for a cheese-with-pickle. The man with the shaven head turned to Clive and me.

'Ah,' he said. 'New faces, I see. And what would you care for, my brothers?'

'Is he related to us?' Clive asked in a whisper.

'No,' I said. 'It's just a manner of speaking.' Then I spoke in my deepest voice. 'Two cheese-and-pickle and two soups'll be fine thanks, mate, no probs.'

'Certainly, brother,' the shaved-head bloke said. 'And may I ask, are you suffering at all from some kind of throat infection? As I can give you the address of a drop-in medical centre where you can get that looked at, if you wish.'

'It's OK, ta,' I said. 'I'm just a bit growly from my years of heavy smoking, but fortunately I've knocked it on the head.'

'Knocked what on the head?' Clive whispered.

'I'll knock you on the head if you don't be quiet,' I told him, and we got our soup and sandwiches, and thanked them kindly (in deep voices) and then returned to our boxes, acting hard and trying to walk like we were forty-five.

'Forty-five, Clive,' I reminded him. 'Not eighty-five.'

'I'll come into your box for breakfast,' he said. And before I could tell him not to, he was in.

'So what are we going to do then?' he said. 'About Dad?'

I told him what I'd been thinking, that there must be someone else who knew the safe combination. Only who?

'Well, I've been doing some thinking too,' Clive said. (Which was unusual for him.) 'And what I thought was, how do we know Dad's still arrested? Maybe they might have let him go by now. Or even cleared his name without us. He might be back managing the hotel and we're out here for nothing.'

I looked at Clive. To be honest, I was shocked. The reason I was shocked was because what he had said made sense.

'That's good thinking, Clive,' I said. (For fair's fair, after all, and praise where it is due.) 'How are we going to find out?'

'Well,' Clive said. 'I don't think we can just walk into the hotel and ask – that would be too risky. Because if Dad isn't back, then we're in trouble. So either we have to sneak in and find out. Or we just phone up and ask to talk to him. And if he's not there, well, we know he's still under arrest.'

'Phone up and ask to talk to him? Did you think of that all on your own, Clive?'

'There's only me here,' he said.

'Did you think of that while you were all alone in your box, in *This Way Up*?'

'Yes, I did,' Clive said. 'I just put on my thinking cap and came up with it.'

'I didn't know you had a thinking cap, Clive. I thought all you had was a baseball cap.'

'It doubles up,' he said.

'OK,' I said. 'Let's finish our soup and sandwiches, give them the mugs back, then let's go find a phone and ring the hotel up.'

'Do we know the number?' Clive asked.

'I've got it here,' I said, rummaging in my pocket and fishing a piece of headed hotel notepaper out, that I'd been using for noughts and crosses. 'Have we got any change for the phone?'

'I think we've got some coins left,' he said, and we had a look between us, and we did. In fact we still had a few pounds in loose change, so we were better off than we thought.

We gave the bald orange people their mugs back, thanked them for the food, then walked off, trying to look and sound like forty-five-year-olds, and went in search of a phone.

'There aren't so many public phones around these days,' Clive said. 'Everyone's got mobiles.'

'We haven't,' I pointed out. 'We left ours in the suite.'

'I hope my box'll be all right in that alleyway,' he said.

'Who'd pinch your box?' I said.

'Someone might,' Clive said. 'I caught some of

those other rough-sleepers looking at *This Way Up* with envious eyes and jealous features.'

'It's all in your mind,' I told him. 'If anyone's got a decent box, it's me. *Fragile* is a collector's item.'

'Yeah, refuse collector's item.'

We saw a phone, which was lucky for Clive, as it spared him a kick in the shins. I rang the number on the hotel notepaper. I got through almost immediately.

'Hotel Royal. Reception desk. How can I help you?'

'Em – I'd like to speak to the manager, please,' I said. 'To Mr Johnson.'

'I'm afraid he's unavailable right now. Would you care to leave a message?'

'Eh, no, it's all right. Can you tell me when he'll be back?'

'I'm afraid I don't have that information at the moment. He could be away for some time. Can I ask who's calling?'

'No. It's OK. I'll call again later.'

I hung up.

'Well?' Clive said.

'He's not there,' I said. 'Still under arrest. They must still think he did it then.'

'So now what do we do?' Clive said.

I thought for a moment.

'It'll have to be Plan B,' I said.

'Plan B?' Clive said. 'Tell me about it. I don't think I know what Plan B is.'

He looked at me expectantly and full of hope. I didn't have the heart to tell him that I didn't know what Plan B was either.

15

Baker Street

It's funny the things you miss when you're sleeping rough: little things, like your pillow. And then bigger things, like your bed. And then there are the things that you would really appreciate a nice long rest from, no matter where you are sleeping – things like Clive.

'Well then,' Clive said. 'So what's Plan B then?'

I would have loved to have soaked in a nice hot bath, and to have washed my face too, and changed my socks, amongst other things. Not that things like that bothered Clive; he'd happily have lived in a cess-pit.

'It's gonna be good, isn't it?' Clive said, as we walked on slowly through the London streets, not thinking of where we were going. 'This Plan B. It's the one, isn't it? Once we implement Plan B, we're going to be sitting pretty on Easy Street. Where is

Easy Street, by the way? Shall we nip into a bookshop and look it up in the *A to Z*?'

'Never mind where Easy Street is, Clive,' I said. 'I don't even know where we are right now. Where have we wandered to?'

We stopped to get our bearings.

'Look,' Clive said, pointing at a long queue of people across the road, all lined up waiting to get into something. 'We're back at the Waxworks.'

'Ah yes, so we are.'

'So what about this Plan B, then?'

As much to distract Clive as from genuine curiosity, I pointed to a newspaper seller on the corner of the road. He was selling copies of the *Evening Standard*, which was a London newspaper that we'd never seen before coming here. They didn't sell it where we lived.

The odd thing about the *Evening Standard* though, is that it comes out in the morning. Even Clive – who is not known for his astuteness or for having much between his ears except bone and gristle – had been drawn to remark on this.

'Here,' he'd said, shortly after we'd arrived at the hotel. 'How come the *Evening Standard* comes out in the morning? Why don't they call it the *Morning Standard* if they're going to bring it out in the morning? And it seems to me that they've got an afternoon edition too. So that ought to be called the *Afternoon Standard*.'

'I quite agree, Clive,' I said. 'It's just sloppy workmanship on someone's part. That's all it is.'

'Exactly,' Clive said. 'They just haven't got any standards.'

'Yes they have,' I said. 'They've got the *Evening Standards*.'

'Having standards in the evening isn't the same as having them all day long though, is it?'

Anyway. As we stood there, opposite the famous Madame Tussaud's Waxworks, I saw scrawled on the announcement sheet by the newspaper seller's kiosk the words: *Five million jewel heist. Film star's jewellery stolen. Man arrested on suspicion.*

'Clive,' I said. 'We need to get a newspaper.'

'Is that Plan B then?' he said. 'Buy a newspaper? Why's that then? Are you going to get a kitten to come and live with you in your box and you need to put some newspaper down until it gets box-trained?'

'Clive – read what it says there.' I pointed to the small placard.

He read it.

'How much money have you got?' he said.

We gathered together enough small change to make the right money, and we went and bought a copy of the paper.

The man who sold them had something of a funny way of talking.

'Gerroor-neeve-ning-han-hard-hneer!' he yelled.

(Which I think translated as 'Get your *Evening Standard* here'.)

I handed over the coins.

'Hair-hoo-hgo-hir!' he said. (Which I think meant 'There you go, sir'.)

'Hank-hoo-herry-hutch!' Clive said. (Which was supposed to mean 'Thank you very much'.)

But instead of the man being pleased to have found someone like Clive who could speak his own kind of language, he got quite hoity-toity and up on his high horse about it.

'Hot-har-hoo-a-halkin-hike-hat-hor?' he said. 'Har-hoo-hrying-hoo-hake-ha-hickey?'

'Hake-ha-hickey?' Clive said, with some indignation. 'Hof-horse-h'I'm-hot-haking-ha-hickey! Hi-hos-hust-hrying-hoo-hee-holite!' (Which I think meant 'Of course I'm not taking the mickey, I was just trying to be polite'.)

But the newspaper seller was not easily placated.

'H'clear-horf!' he said. 'Ha-hore-hi-hick-hoor-hackshide!'

As neither of us wanted a hick in the hackshide, we took our paper and we h'cleared-horf sharpish.

'Come on then,' Clive said. 'What does it say?'

There it was, all over the front page, and over three of the inside pages as well: the whole story of the vanished jewellery, how it had mysteriously gone from the Hotel Royal safe.

Then, on the inside pages, were photos of Daphne

Spurter arriving for her premiere at the cinema in Leicester Square, surrounded by fans and bodyguards, but minus her jewellery. In the background we could make out Mrs Swanker Watson too – although some of the sparkle had gone out of her usual swank, as she didn't have her jewellery with her either.

'Listen to this, Clive,' I said, reading from the inside page. '*A man has been held in custody overnight, and is believed to be continuing to help the police with their enquiries. Sources say that formal charges will be made within the next twenty-four hours.*'

Clive looked very pale again; his lower lip was trembling.

'Dad,' he said. 'They've locked him up.'

'We already knew that, Clive.'

'I know, but it seems worse reading about it in the papers.'

Clive got more and more agitated and started biting at his pullover sleeve, which is a nasty habit he's got when he's worked up about something. It's especially unpleasant when he gets into that state but isn't wearing his pullover, as he will then start to bite at *your* sleeves instead.

'We've got to get Dad out,' he said. 'We've got to get Dad out of jail.'

'That's what we're doing, Clive. That's just what we're trying to do.'

'It's bad enough not having a mum, I couldn't

bear not to have a dad as well . . .'

'Clive, calm down. I've got a plan.' (And I really had now. It had come to me when I realized where we were standing. But I'll explain that in a moment.)

'We've got to spring him' Clive said. 'We've got to help him break out of jail.'

'We can't do that, Clive. Be sensible. There's just two of us. We're still at school. How can we help Dad break out of jail?'

'We get a cake,' Clive said, getting more and more hyper. 'That's it, we bake a cake, and we put a file inside it.'

'And then what?'

'And then . . . and then . . . we eat the cake, get the file out, post it to Dad in a Jiffy bag, and then he'll be out in a jiffy – no . . . no wait . . .'

'Clive!' I said sharply. 'Pull yourself together! You're getting hysterical! You're losing it. Look at your sleeves! They're all bitten and covered in slavers!'

'But we have to do something, we have to, we have, we—'

'CLIVE!'

He finally shut up.

'No need to shout at me,' he said.

'Clive,' I said. 'I think I know who did it.'

He went very quiet then, and he looked at me very suspiciously.

'How – how can you possibly know that?'

'Look, Clive,' I said. 'Look where we are.'

'Where?'

I pointed at the Underground station sign across the way.

'Baker Street,' I said. 'And who used to live in Baker Street?'

'Eh – Mr Bun the Baker?' Clive said.

'No, Clive. A famous detective.'

'Mr Bun the Detective then?'

'Clive, don't you ever read any books?'

'Course I do. I read a book a week.'

'Clive, the *Beano* is not a book.'

'All right. So who did live in Baker Street then?'

'Sherlock Holmes, the famous detective.'

'But he wasn't real. How's he going to help us?'

'His methods, Clive.'

'Did he have methods then?'

'Of course he had methods. You can't solve crimes if you don't have methods.'

'Was he methodical in his methods then? I mean, what were his methods exactly?'

'His methods were, Clive, that once you have eliminated every other possibility, what remains, no matter how improbable it may seem, has to be the solution.'

'And what does that mean?'

'Clive. The safe could only have been opened by someone who had the combination. Dad had the combination, but we know Dad didn't do it. Mrs

Dominics must have the combination too. But we know she wouldn't do it either. So that leaves only one possible answer.'

'What?'

'Clive – think about it!'

'. . . Yeah?'

'Clive, we've got to find Mrs Dominics. We need to talk to her. We've got to find out where she lives, get in to see her, and tell her what's happened.'

'She'll already know, won't she? Someone will have told her. Or she'll have seen the news.'

'Maybe, yes, probably. But we need her help to prove that Dad's innocent.'

'Can't we go to the police?'

'Clive, the police are after us, remember? To take us into Care. They're not going to listen to us, a couple of kids of our age. They won't listen to our theories of who really did it and how to catch them. They'll just think we're a couple of upset kids who can't accept that their dad's a crook. They won't listen to us and they won't do anything, except lock us up in a home or send us to live with foster parents who'll make us sleep in a cardboard box—'

'I don't mind that,' Clive said. 'I'm getting quite fond of my cardboard box.'

'Or they'll send us to live with Grandma and Granddad, and his corduroy trousers.'

Clive went paler than pale.

'Not,' he said, 'the corduroy trousers.'

'He might even buy us a pair each, and we'll have to wear them – and corduroy swimming trunks too, for when we go swimming – and there we'll be, all three of us, in corduroy trousers. And corduroy socks too, probably, and corduroy shoes and corduroy underpants. And we'll have to sleep in a corduroy bed!'

'It's more than flesh and blood can bear!' Clive said. 'It's more than skin and bone can take. So what do we have to do?'

'We have to get to see Mrs Dominics. We have to find her address – the address of her mansion in the country.'

'And where are we going to find that?'

'In the manager's office,' I said, 'of the Hotel Royal. It'll be there, in Dad's address book.'

'What if the police have taken it away?'

'That's a risk we have to take. If it's gone, Mrs Dominics's address will be on file somewhere else. We'll find it.'

'So you mean – we have to sneak back . . . into the hotel . . . into the very manager's office . . . where the safe is . . . get the address book . . . and get back out again . . . without being seen?'

'You have smacked the nail firmly on the cranium, Clive,' I said, 'with the blunt instrument of your brain.'

'Eh?' he said.

'Never mind.'

'So how do we do it then?' Clive said, as we turned round and walked back the way we had come, back towards Piccadilly and the Hotel Royal. 'How do we get into the hotel and out again without being seen? How do we do it, eh? I bet you've got a plan, haven't you? I bet you've got a *really* good plan. Haven't you? This is Plan C, now, isn't it?'

'Eh, that's right, Clive,' I nodded. 'We'll implement Plan C.'

'And so what is Plan C exactly then?' Clive asked.

'Tell you what, Clive,' I said. 'It's a few minutes' walk until we get there. Why don't you tell me what you think it is?'

'Plan C, eh?'

'Plan C.'

'All right then. Give me a moment.'

He thought long, and he thought hard, as we went along. You could tell it from the expression on his face, which had taken on the look of a peeled walnut. We'd walked as far as the bottom of the Tottenham Court Road, the bit where all the computer shops are, when Clive looked up from his trainers, which he had been staring at as he shuffled along.

'I've got it,' he said. 'I know what you've got in mind. Plan C goes like this . . .'

16

Plan C

Clive had worked out Plan C just as I had imagined it.

I felt it was good that I was there to give him guidance on the matter of plans, and a chance to work the basics out for himself, for otherwise Clive would never have developed his planning skills.

Clive is always being sent on little courses at school during the lunch hour to improve his various skills (and/or his lack of them). He has had special tuition for his bicycling skills, his eating-without-spilling-it-all-over-yourself skills, his not-making-smells-in-class skills, his keeping-your-finger-out-of-your-nose skills, and his trying-to-acquire-some-skills skills.

That is not to say that Clive doesn't have any natural skills at all, as he does, but these are mostly of an antisocial nature. I sometimes fear that if Clive does not work hard on his staying-out-of-prison skills, that is where he will end up. And unlike Dad, he'll be in there for something he has done – unless he works on his mistaken-identity skills and his hire-a-good-lawyer skills, which I can't see him bothering to do, due to his over-developed couch-potato skills.

'OK,' Clive said. 'I've worked out Plan C. I know just what you're thinking.'

'Go on then, Clive,' I said. 'Hit me with it.'

'Hit you with what?' he said, his eyes lighting up. It was a mistake to use an expression like that. Clive is always on the lookout for a free hit, and I should never have mentioned one.

'Hit me with Plan C,' I said, 'is what I mean.'

'But it's not solid. Shall I write it all down on a plank first?'

'Clive—'

'OK. Here's what you thought of. Your plan is that we should go back to the hotel, sneak into the staff locker room, pinch a couple of porters' jackets and a couple of name badges, smarm our hair down with a few dollops of gel or a drop of olive oil from the kitchen, and then head for the lobby.'

'Go on, Clive,' I said. 'You're sort of on the right lines.'

'We got away with being waiters,' Clive continued, 'so we ought to get away with being porters. Or bell-boys even. If you can be a bus-boy, then you can be a bell-boy too. It's just a matter of having the clapper for it.'

'So what if somebody stops us, Clive, and challenges us? What's your plan for that?'

'Ah, well now, I've got a sort of sub-plan for that,' he said. 'A kind of Plan C Plus. If anyone stops us, we pretend that we can't understand them. We pretend that we can't speak much English, so we ignore them, walk off, and then run like hell once we're round the corner. If they see us running, they'll just think we're illegal immigrants. If they stop us and we get caught, we'll claim political asylum in foreign accents. When we do that, no one will want to be bothered with all the paperwork, so they'll let us escape.'

'Sounds pretty watertight so far,' I said encouragingly.

'Was it what you were thinking?' Clive said.

'Pretty much,' I nodded. 'Pretty much so. Bar one or two small details.'

Clive looked a bit downcast at that.

'Cor,' he said. 'I wish I could think of plans the way you can. If only I could think of plans too. If I could do that, I'd be able to make something of myself and be a success in life. But I can't think of any plans at all.'

'Try not to worry, Clive,' I commiserated. 'I'm sure there's other things you're good at – stuff like being a shoe-shine boy, and delivering door-to-door horse dung from a hand-cart. The kinds of things where plans aren't so important.'

'Yes,' Clive said, in a bit of a subdued and dismal way. 'I can think of schemes, sometimes and the occasional sneaky plot, but a plan, well – where would you start? Still, never mind. Even if I do end up as a shoe-shine boy, at least I'll see life.'

'Not really, Clive,' I pointed out. 'You'll just see feet mostly.'

'What do you think you'll be when you grow up?' Clive asked.

'Probably a brain surgeon, I guess, Clive,' I told him. 'Or maybe I'll become a famous chef.'

'I wouldn't mind being a chef too,' Clive said.

'You can't cook, Clive,' I pointed out.

'No,' he said. 'But I'm ******* good at swearing.'

'So what do you think the rest of my plan is then, Clive?' I said, wondering if he'd figured it all out. 'Just out of interest. Just to see that you've got the whole thing right.'

'OK,' Clive said. 'Here's what we do. We hang around the lobby in our porters' uniforms, waiting until the coast is clear. One of us stands guard outside the manager's office while the other one nips in, looks through the filing cabinets, gets Mrs Dominics's address, or at least her phone number, then out he comes, we head back for the staff room, get rid of the jackets, and away.'

There was a lull in the conversation as we walked

along and as I pondered what Clive had said.

'So is that right?' he asked. 'Is that your Plan C?'

'Indeed it is, Clive,' I said. 'That's the very one.'

He seemed more downcast than ever then, did Clive. A look of deep depression and woe came over him.

'Cor, I do wish I could think of plans,' he said. 'Only I never will.'

'Don't take it to heart, Clive,' I said. 'It's just how things are. The man upstairs giveth, Clive,' I said, 'and the man upstairs taketh away.'

'What man upstairs?' he said. 'Has he got a shop up there?'

'I'm talking in parables, Clive,' I said.

'If you ask me, you're talking ****!' Clive said, and he stomped off ahead of me.

Personally I blamed Gilbert Rimsey.

That and Clive not being able to think of plans. It seemed to have put him in a bit of a strop.

We were back at the alley. Some of the rough-sleepers were still curled up in their boxes. The trouble with sleeping rough is that you never get much sleep. You're always being woken up by the cold, or the discomfort, or by someone bringing soup and sandwiches round, or by some policeman or security guard, wanting to know what you're up to – though it's obvious that what you're up to is sleeping. As a result of this, you're half tired all day long, and try to snatch a few moments' rest whenever you can.

'Hey! Look!' Clive said indignantly. 'Someone's been at my box.'

They had too. Some stick-it-up-your-pullover-sized bits of cardboard had been torn from his box. Somebody must have snaffled them to use as insulation, or a temporary vest. Instead of *This Way Up*, his box now read *Way Up*. Someone had had a piece of my box too. Instead of *Fragile*, I was *agile*.

Barnsley glowered at us from inside his box. I realized that he was the tinned tomatoes I had nearly stepped on the night before.

'I bet it was him,' Clive whispered.

I agreed, but he was a bit hairy and grumpy-looking, with a thick, matted beard, which probably doubled up as a wildlife preserve and a haven for endangered species – mostly of the flea variety – so I decided not to complain.

'Just ignore him,' I said. 'Don't make an issue of it.'

But Barnsley wasn't as willing to let us pass without remark.

'Disgusting,' he said.

'Beg pardon?' I said.

'Two youngsters like you, with your whole lives ahead of you, sleeping rough at your age!'

'We're down on our luck,' Clive said.

'Don't matter,' Barnsley said. 'There's no call for

youngsters of your age rough-sleeping. Different for me. I was hit hard by life. I used to be a successful businessman once, with my own bucket and ladder.'

'What line were you in?' Clive asked.

'Window cleaning! What else would I be in, with a bucket and a ladder? I'd hardly be a chartered accountant or a barrister, would I?'

'You haven't got the lid of my box up your jumper, have you?' Clive said, but I nudged him not to pursue the matter.

'I had it all once,' Barnsley continued. 'Business, home, family, car, money, holidays, ironing board, bed, digital radio, some envelopes, a stapler, season ticket for the football – all the things that money can buy. But then I fell ill, couldn't work for a while, started drinking, my wife left me and took the kids with her, I couldn't pay the mortgage, I started drinking even more, I lost the house and everything else and now here I am, in a cardboard box, by the side of the Hotel Royal. But you, you're young lads. You haven't even started, but you've already given up.'

'It's not as it seems,' I said. 'We've been brought low by circumstances outside our control. Once we had it all too, and we lived in luxury penthouse suites and travelled on the finest cruise liners, enjoying first-class service and gourmet dinners and fine wines—'

'Ah, pull the other one, it's got bells on,' he said.

And with that, he closed the lid of his box on us and refused to continue the conversation.

It's always the same, it seems to me. Grown-ups go on at you to tell the truth, but when you do, they don't believe a word of it.

We went on to the end of the alley. From there a very narrow lane ran along the rear of the hotel to come out by the staff entrance in the car park.

We left our stuff hidden under the fire escape gantry, and headed along the lane.

I got out my baseball hat and pulled it low over my eyes. Clive did the same with his. It looked as if he had a beak.

'OK, Clive,' I said. 'Let's do it. And remember – softly, softly, catchee monkey.'

He looked blank.

'Are we after monkeys now?' he said. 'I thought we were—'

'I mean proceed with caution, Clive,' I said. 'There's no sense in spoiling the ship for a ha'penny worth of tar.'

'Got it,' he said. 'You're speaking foreign and pretending to be an illegal immigrant, aren't you?'

We saw the staff door open and someone come out and walk away.

We darted from the lane, ran across the tarmac, and Clive grabbed the self-locking door before it closed.

We made it through, and the door clicked shut behind us.

We'd done it. We were in.

We were back in the Hotel Royal. Only this time not as the acting manager's sons, not as revered and honoured guests. This time, as humble porters and as wanted men on the run.

Luck was with us.

We headed for the locker room. There were plenty of people milling around, of all shapes, sizes and nationalities. Posh hotels and restaurants couldn't keep going without foreign and immigrant workers. Some of them were smaller than us, and some of them even looked younger, though they were maybe about fifty-five. It's funny the way different nationalities age. Some people hardly seem to grow old for ages and ages, then they suddenly get ancient overnight. If anyone spoke to us, we answered with some friendly-sounding gibberish.

'Morning.'

'Chakabuchka,' Clive said. (Clive is good at talking gibberish as he has spoken it for most of his life.)

We found a selection of porters' uniforms hanging up on the freshly laundered rack.

'What size?'

'Small and pigeon-like about the chest and big around the bum for you, Clive,' I said. 'And manly about the chest and snake-like about the hips for me.'

'But we take the same sizes,' Clive objected.

217

'Just grab one and get it on!'

We put the uniforms on, leaving our own stuff in a locker. The porters in the Hotel Royal wore hats as well as jackets – black sort of pillbox hats with the hotel name embroidered on them in gold thread.

'How do I look?' Clive asked.

'Like a bell-hop,' I said.

'Convincing?'

'It'll do. What about me?'

'Looks all right.'

'Right then. Let's go.'

'Wait – what about name badges? Won't look right without name badges.'

Clive was right. Everyone who worked in the hotel wore a name badge. There was a box of them in the locker room, old ones by the look of it, left by people who were off-duty, or who'd moved on and didn't work there any more.

'Here.' I handed him a badge.

'Spongo?' he said. 'What sort of name is that?'

'It doesn't matter. Come on.' I grabbed a badge for myself. It had *Drongo* written on it.

'Drongo and Spongo?' Clive said. 'Who were they? Where did they come from? The circus?'

'It doesn't matter. Now, come on, Clive. Let's go.'

We left the staff room and stepped out into the corridor.

As we did, a huge man with a barrel chest, dressed in a splendid uniform adorned with gold braid, came striding along. I recognized him from our penthouse days. He was the top man, the head porter. His name badge said as much, and under the title *Head Porter* was the word *Bruno*.

He spotted us.

'Oi! You two!' he boomed. 'You! It's you, I mean. The two little porter chappies! Pongo and Stumpo or whoever you are. I want you!'

I could sense Clive's legs trembling, and they weren't even in my shoes.

'Front lobby! Now! There's not a bell-hop in sight. So get out there. Hop some bells and carry some cases. And get a move on! Go! At the double.'

We nodded meekly and hurried on our way. We pushed open another door, which led from the backstairs staff section to the hotel proper.

'We fooled him, Clive,' I whispered. 'We must look like proper porters, eh?'

'It's not Clive, it's Spongo!' he hissed.

We hurried on, heads down, trying to look anonymous, making our way towards the front lobby.

It was all going fine until we passed the main staircase, when a voice called out. And it was plainly aimed at us.

'Porter!' the voice said. 'I say, porter! I need a porter!'

It was Mrs Swanker Watson.

17

At the Wheel

'You there,' she said. 'Yes, you there. You two. Snorky and Porky or whatever your names are. You'll do. We are leaving this hotel and we need our bags brought down. Room five-one-six. See to it, would you? Thank you very much. I'll tip you later.'

She swanked off in the direction of the lobby desk.

'Cor,' Clive said, as we watched her go. 'Tips. Maybe we ought to forget about being detectives and stick to the portering lark.'

Mrs Swanker banged on the bell and spoke loudly to the receptionist on duty.

'Bill, please,' she said. 'Mr and Mrs Watson. But don't think I'm going to pay it. Not until my jewellery has been found. This hotel's negligence has been responsible for absolutely ruining our holiday. That and your dishonest manager. They

221

were family heirlooms, those jewels of mine. Worth half a million at the least . . .'

I was a bit suspicious when I heard that, thinking that perhaps Mrs Swanker was exaggerating the value of her stolen jewels and that there was more than one crook about the place.

She turned to see me and Clive still standing there, hovering in the background and waiting for her to go away so that we could sneak into the manager's office.

'Haven't you gone yet?' she snapped. 'You two! Spingy and Spongy, or whoever. Room five-one-six. Choppy-choppy.'

'Better do as she wants,' Clive said, 'or we won't get our tips.'

'Tips, Clive!' I said indignantly. 'We're not here for tips! We're here to clear Dad's name and to see justice is done and to bring the guilty parties to book.'

'Yeah,' he said, 'but if we can make a bit of money while we're doing it—'

'You two!' Mrs Swanker snapped. 'Are you porters or do you just stand around making the place look untidy?'

I could see that if we didn't go, there was going to be trouble.

'OK, Clive,' I said. 'Come on. Let's get it over with and then we can do what we came here for.'

So we grabbed a luggage trolley, wheeled it

to the lift, and went up to the fifth floor.

When we knocked on the door of room five-one-six, it was opened by Swanker. He peered at us with curiosity and suspicion, looking from our name badges to our faces, to our pillbox hats, and back again.

'We ha come to takea cases 'way,' Clive said, in a strange, high-pitched, strangled tone, which made him sound like some kind of vaguely Chinese Eskimo with Scandinavian connections.

'Drongo and Spongo?' Swanker said, reading the name badges. 'You don't half remind me of someone.'

'Swanker,' I said, closing the door behind us. 'It's us. Me and Clive.'

'Flipping heck,' Swanker said. 'So it is. What are you doing here, dressed up as hospital orderlies?'

'Porters!'

'And why has Clive got a greasy head? And why is he wearing a hat like a big aspirin?'

'Don't be stupid,' I said. 'Clive's always got a greasy head.'

'Not that greasy. But what are you doing here? Everyone's looking for you. They reckon your dad pinched the jewellery.'

'He never did.'

'No, I didn't think so, but that's what they reckon. The evidence is against him.'

'Well, we're here to clear his name – which is why

we're undercover. But your mum spotted us and nabbed us to shift your cases.'

'Yeah, we're going home,' Swanker said dismally. 'She's upset about her jewels, and Dad's gone back to drowning his sorrows.'

A loud snore came from one of the bedrooms, and I got a glimpse through the partially opened door of Mr Swanker Watson asleep on the bed, with his arms around a whisky bottle – which looked very empty.

'Sorry, Swanker,' I said, as we grabbed the suitcases which had been left out and stacked them onto the trolley. 'Sorry if it's ruined your holiday, but we have to clear our dad's name. We'll get your mum's stuff back, don't you worry. I don't know how yet, but we will.'

'We'll do it with Plan D,' Clive said.

'Great! What is Plan D?' Swanker asked him.

'It's confidential,' Clive explained.

'Ah, right then.'

There was the sound of restless stirrings from the bedroom, as if Mr Swanker was waking like a bear from hibernation – a bear with a very sore head.

'OK, that's it, last one, Clive,' I said, as I piled the last of the suitcases on board the trolley. 'You won't say you've seen us, will you, Swanker?'

'Not me,' he said. 'I hope you manage to clear your dad's name.'

'Thanks, Swank,' I said. 'We appreciate it. Better

224

go then, before we run into your mum again and she realizes who we are.'

'Right.'

Swanker looked round then, to see that Clive was standing in front of him, looking at him expectantly, with his hand held out.

'What do you want?' Swanker said.

'My tip,' Clive told him.

'Tip?'

'Yeah. Your mum promised us a tip for collecting the cases.'

'Then you'd better see her about that then, hadn't you?' Swanker said.

'Swanker,' Clive said, 'you're mean and tight-fisted.'

'Yes but—'

'Come on,' Clive said. 'Let's be on our way. I can see we'll get no tips here.'

He pushed the trolley out of the room.

'Sorry, Swank,' I said. 'We'll be seeing you.'

It seems to me sometimes that I spend a lot of my time apologizing for Clive and his behaviour. I don't think he appreciates it.

I caught up with him at the lift, punching the call button impatiently.

'It knows we're waiting, Clive. You've pressed it once. Pressing it again and again won't help.'

'This is ridiculous. We'll be waiting here all day. I'm taking the stairs,' he said.

'No, Clive,' I said. 'I don't think that's a very good idea.'

He set off with the trolley and I went after him. We stopped at the top of the staircase. It was a long way down to the next landing, and there were four more flights below that.

'Here we go then,' Clive said. 'Hop on. We ought to make it. I think I can probably steer it as we go.'

'No, Clive,' I said, and I grabbed hold of the trolley to stop him launching it off.

'Geronimo! We have lift-off!'

I was already too late. It was a matter of jump on board the trolley or get dragged down after it. I took the first option and jumped on, joining Clive and the suitcases.

'Wheeee!' Clive yelled. 'This is all right, isn't it! This is better than Alton Towers!'

Now, I don't know if you have ever ridden a hotel luggage trolley down five flights of stairs, along with a big stack of suitcases and a nutcase in a porter's uniform wearing a name badge with *Spongo* on it, but it is not what you would call relaxing.

It was an especially tense moment when we came to the first turn in the staircase.

'Clive!' I yelled. 'We're going to smash into the wall!'

'Never!' he said, and he managed to wrench the front of the trolley round.

We took the first landing on two wheels, slowed

slightly on the flat, and then we were off again, down the next flight of stairs, heading for the third floor.

It is hard to convey – now that some time has gone by and recollection has dimmed – the expressions of astonishment, not to say terror, that I saw on the faces of those we passed. But one elderly couple on the second-floor landing will remain etched for ever in my mind. They managed to throw themselves against the wall just in time to avoid total squashing.

'Flipping pedestrians,' Clive said. 'Don't they ever look where they're going?'

The final flight was the worst and the longest. It was a straight run down to the corridor, and from the bottom of the stairs to the lobby was about fifty metres.

Clive reckons that by that time we must have been doing about sixty miles an hour. Personally, I would put it at nearer eighty. Whatever the truth of the matter, we hit that corridor in a blur. Had the floor been tiles or polished wood, we'd have kept going and shot straight out of the revolving doors, right into the mid-morning traffic, and all the way down Piccadilly, probably ending up in Fortnum and Mason's, the swanky department store.

As it was, luck and deep-pile carpets were on our side. The thick, heavy carpet slowed us down, and we drifted to a halt by a pillar in the lobby – just behind Mrs Swanker Watson, who was still at the reception desk, arguing about her bill and blaming the hotel for losing her jewellery.

She must have heard the rattle and the *whoosh* as we arrived with her luggage. She turned and looked at us.

'So what kept you?' she said.

There's no pleasing some people.

Clive put his hand out for a tip, and I did the same, feeling that if I didn't Mrs Swanker would become suspicious and realize that we were not proper porters at all – for porters who do not want their tips are unknown in the world.

'There you are.'

'Thank you.'

'I'd give you more,' Mrs Swanker said pointedly, 'only I can't afford to, as I've had my jewellery stolen!'

She went back to arguing with the people behind the desk. It took everyone on duty to deal with her, as Mrs Swanker is not a woman to be crossed when it comes to her jewellery. But this was good for us. It meant that everybody was distracted, and we were free to get into the manager's office.

'Clive,' I said. 'Now's our chance. Come on.'

We were across the lobby in a couple of shakes, into the manager's office, and closing the door behind us.

'Can you lock it?'

'No key,' Clive said.

'Then just stand guard while I look.'

I began to pull open drawers and filing cabinets and to rifle through them, looking for Dad's address book, but it wasn't there. I guessed that the police had already searched the office and taken much of the stuff with them.

'Come on, come on – someone'll come in and want to know what we're doing here.'

'Wait . . .'

I yanked open the bottom drawer of the filing cabinet.

'*Staff Details*.'

I took the folder out.

'What are you doing?' Clive said. 'I thought all you wanted was Mrs Dominics's address.'

'I want this too,' I said, as I extracted a paper from one of the *Staff Detail* files and shoved it into my pocket.

'What do you want that for?'

'You'll see.'

'Come on, come on,' Clive said. He was still by the door, holding it open a fraction, so that he could see out. 'The row's easing off. Mrs Swanker's running out of steam.'

I still needed to find Mrs Dominics's' address. It had to be there. It was just a matter of where.

'Come on,' Clive said. 'Come on. Hurry up! There's someone coming!'

I pulled open another drawer. I found another

file, labelled *Shareholders, A-list Visitors & VIPs.*

There it was – Mrs Dominics's country address. I tore it out and stuffed it into my pocket, replaced the file, and slammed the drawer shut, just as—

'What are you two doing in here!'

The door opened.

It was another porter, one of the senior ones, with two stripes on his arm, the one called Lester – the same one we'd encountered at the back of the hotel on the day we had arrived, who had called our car a dinky-mobile.

'What are you doing? This is the manager's office. You shouldn't be in here.'

'We . . . we . . . came in by histake-ski,' Clive said, in his Spongo voice.

Lester looked at us through narrowed eyes.

'I know you,' he said.

'No hugh don't-ski,' Clive said. 'Hugh jus htink hugh do. A lotta pweople htink that. But dwere wong.'

'Well, you shouldn't be in here, so move. The light board's going mad out there with people wanting porters, so go and do what you're paid for. Get on with it. Because I'm off-duty now. Move.'

'Wright away!' Clive said, and we hurried out under his baleful gaze. He carefully scrutinized our name badges as we passed.

'Spongo and Drongo, eh? Foreign, are you?'

'Hyes,' Clive said. 'We from Scotland hin the Glen.'

I shoved him out of the door before he could say anything else. Lester stayed in the office, probably to check that nothing had been disturbed.

'Go, and keep going,' I said. 'To the staff room and out the back!'

'Porter! I say, porter!'

A voice boomed across the lobby and a red-faced man who had just arrived waved at us to help him with his cases.

'With you in a moment, sir,' I said. 'Just have a job to do.'

But it wasn't a job that we were on.

It was a mission.

We walked swiftly, heads down, stopping for no one. We pushed the *Staff Only* door open and walked past the kitchens of the Royal Grill.

'Call those ******* vegetables washed?' I heard Gilbert Rimsey shouting at someone. 'I've seen cleaner horse droppings!'

We got to the locker room, changed into our own things, and headed for the rear door, to take us out to the car park.

'Now what?' Clive said.

'Mrs Dominics,' I said. 'We'll go and see her.'

'Where does she live?'

I showed Clive the address.

'So where's that?'

'About thirty miles outside of London.'

'And how do we get there?'

'Get the train, I suppose.'

'What do we pay for the tickets with?'

That was a good point. How did we pay for them? We didn't have enough left for more than a couple of burgers.

'Perhaps we can sneak onto the train and then hide in the toilet to avoid the ticket inspector?'

'Not a chance, Clive,' I said. 'You can't even get onto the platform without a ticket these days.'

'Then how do we get there?'

'Let me think . . .'

I was thinking hard when I got a nudge in the ribs from an elbow.

'Look,' Clive said.

'What?'

'Our car's still there in the car park.'

'So?'

'We could have slept in it, instead of roughing it in those boxes.'

'How? It's locked and Dad's got the key.'

'Yeah, but there's the spare, remember? Remember that time we lost the key and got stuck miles from anywhere? And he said never again. So he got another spare cut and put it in a little magnetic box under the back bumper – where no one would know it was there but us.'

'Yeah, but that doesn't help us now, does it, Clive? It's not somewhere to sleep we need right now, it's transport.'

'But I thought – a car was transport.'

'Yes, Clive. It's transport all right – but only if you have a driver.'

Sometimes Clive's lack of the basics in the brains department makes me all but despair.

'But we do have a driver,' he said.

'Who?'

'Me,' he said.

I stared at him.

'You?'

He reached into his pocket and took out a card. He unfolded it and showed it to me.

This is to certify, it read, *that Clive Johnson has passed his Legoland driving test, and is allowed to drive all Lego cars at Legoland Theme Parks around the world.*

'See,' he said.

'Clive,' I said. 'That is a licence for driving a Lego car. Our car is not a Lego car. Our car is a proper car, with gears and a petrol engine and all the rest. It's not a little electrical buggy!'

'Same difference,' Clive said. 'I reckon I could do it.'

If I'd had any choice, I would never have agreed to it. But as it was, I didn't see that there was any alternative. Sometimes it's necessary to break the law in little ways in order to stop a greater injustice being done. We had to prove that Dad was innocent and we couldn't do it alone. We needed a grown-up who would listen to us and believe us, and the only one I could think of was Mrs D. A phone call wouldn't have done it either. We had to see her. We had to talk to her in person, and nobody else.

'OK, Clive,' I said. 'Under normal circumstances I would rather go bungee-jumping without a bungee whilst juggling with razor blades than get into a car with you at the wheel. But there's no choice. So you drive, and I'll navigate. Put your baseball hat on and pull it down a bit so nobody can see that you don't look old enough to be driving. And let's go.'

Clive went and got the spare key from where Dad had hidden it, in the little magnetic box on the chassis behind the rear bumper.

'Don't you worry,' he said. 'I'll have us there in no time. I mean, you saw the way I steered that luggage trolley down five flights of stairs, didn't you?'

'Not entirely, Clive,' I said. 'I had my eyes closed for most of it.'

'Well, for luggage trolley, read car. Same deal, only faster.'

'I think I might sit in the back, Clive,' I said. 'And then I'll be able to wear two seatbelts.'

'No,' he said. 'I'll need you next to me to navigate.'

We got in and put our seatbelts on. Clive turned the key in the ignition.

'Are you sure you know what you're doing, Clive?' I said.

'Not really,' he said. 'But it's never stopped me before.'

With that he fired the engine up, let off the handbrake, like he'd seen Dad do, put his foot down, and we took off, bouncing and kangarooing at considerable speed.

'Slow down a bit, Clive,' I said. 'Don't forget there's a barrier.'

'Don't worry about it,' he said. 'It'll open automatically. Relax and enjoy the ride,' he said. 'And we'll be there in no time. Just close your eyes and take it easy, same as me.'

We didn't actually get quite as far as Clive said we would. No, we didn't make it even half the way to Mrs Dominics's house.

In fairness to Clive though, I must admit that he was right about the barrier opening automatically. Unfortunately, however, it opened not because we were going out, but because another car was coming in.

'Remind me,' Clive said, when he saw the other car approaching. 'Which of these pedals is the brake again?'

'I'll look it up for you in the handbook,' I offered. 'Hold on while I get it out of the glove compartment.'

No, we didn't make it all the way to Mrs Dominics's place.

But we almost got out of the car park.

18

A Small Dent

Clive still maintains, to this day, that if you are going to drive into the front of another car, then the best car to drive into is a Rolls Royce. He says that if you do have to put dents in bumpers, it is best to do it in style.

We had actually slowed down somewhat when we crashed into Mrs Dominics's Rolls Royce. It too was going at a leisurely pace, nosing its way into the hotel car park as the barrier ascended and as we came out.

A Rolls Royce is quite a big car – at least it certainly was compared to ours – but for all its size, its looming bonnet and shining chrome, its most distinguishing and memorable characteristic at that moment was two huge soup plates which turned out, upon closer inspection, to be Chaswick the chauffeur's eyeballs.

'What the—' I seemed to hear him call, and he used a few of those choice words which were such an essential ingredient of Gilbert Rimsey's cooking.

Then there was the crash. We came to a halt immediately.

'Cor!' Clive said. 'That was a close one.'

'Clive,' I pointed out to him, 'that wasn't a close one. That *was* one!'

We couldn't immediately see the extent of the damage because the bonnet of our car had flipped up over the windscreen. I could hear what sounded like water spewing out of the radiator, and the *tinkle-tinkle* of fast-moving car parts as they rolled away in all directions. The bonnet suddenly fell back down again with a loud *bang*, leaving us with a clear view of the scene.

'What do we do now?' Clive said. 'How's about we amble away casually, whistling a careless tune, and pretending we had nothing to do with it?'

'Bit late for that, Clive,' I said, pointing out of the window at the purple face heading towards us. The face – like our radiator – seemed to have large quantities of steam coming out of it.

'Oh look,' Clive said. 'It's old Chaswick coming over to say hello. And that looks like Mrs Dominics in the back of the car. I dare say old Chaswick is coming over to apologize for crashing into us, and to give us his insurance particulars so as we can make a claim for the damage.'

'Don't,' I said to Clive, 'bank on it.'

I could hear the scrunch of broken glass as Chaswick walked towards us. It sounded like somebody walking on bags of crisps.

'Shall I wind down the window?' Clive asked. 'And give him the old soft word that turneth away wrath, like they told us about in religious studies?'

'I wouldn't advise it, Clive,' I said. 'Best to lock the doors, I think, and then sneak out of the boot and run for it at the first opportunity. That way we'll avoid the big fist that handeth out pain.'

Clive just managed to hit the central-locking button in time. Chaswick was upon us.

'You in there!' he yelled. 'What the Gilbert Rimsey do you think you're doing? Don't you ever look where you're going? Haven't you got any Gilbert Rimsey brakes in that Gilbert Rimsey dinky-mobile? Why don't you buy yourself a pair of Gilbert Rimsey glasses so you can see where you're Gilbert going! Are you sure you've got a Rimsey Gilbert licence!'

I think that initially the sun was in his eyes, reflecting off our front windscreen, and so he didn't at first see inside the car, nor realize who was sitting behind the wheel. But the mists cleared and the penny dropped as Chaswick pressed his nose up against the driver's window and peered inside to see Clive in his baseball hat, trying to look like a real motorist.

'Gilbert Rimsey me!' he said. 'It's Gilbert Rimsey

you two! What the Gilbert Rimsey are you doing behind the wheel of that Gilbert Rimsey car!'

In circumstances such as these – as I have often explained to Clive – it is best not to exchange light-hearted banter nor to give expression to words which may only inflame an already overheated situation and be as the petrol to the fire. It is always best to look humble and contrite and to say as little as possible – with the possible exception of 'Sorry'.

'Open that Gilbert Rimsey door!' Chaswick said in a sharp tone. 'I want to come in there and tear your Gilbert Rimsey head off your Gilbert Rimsey shoulders.'

'He's taking a bit of a strong line out there, isn't he, Clive?' I said. 'Very forceful.'

'Yes,' Clive said. 'And after all – accidents happen.'

Chaswick banged on the window again with his fist.

'What do you think you're doing, you two vandals? You shouldn't be in that car! You don't even have a licence between you!'

In order to correct him on this point, Clive got out his Legoland Lego car licence, smoothed it out and held it up against the window for Chaswick to see.

He stood, peering down, to read it. His lips forming the words as he read them.

'Legoland . . . Lego car . . . what the Gilbert Rimsey is that!'

Clive turned to look at me.

'How about I hit the ejector-seat button?' he said.

'I think you'll find, Clive,' I said, 'that our car doesn't have one.'

'Maybe we could tell him we've got urgent dental appointments then . . .'

'The way things are going,' I said, 'if he gets his hands on us, we'll be needing urgent dental appointments.'

The car started to rock. It was Chaswick. I wasn't sure if he was trying to wrench the door open, or if he wanted to flip the whole car over, get it onto its back, and then stamp on it.

We were saved by the approach of elderly footsteps.

'What is it, Chaswick? Is there a problem? They're not injured in the other car, are they?'

'Not yet,' Chaswick said. 'But give me a few minutes, ma'am, and I'll see what I can do.'

It was Mrs Dominics. She looked inside the car and saw who it was.

'Boys! It's you! Good heavens, how glad I am to see you! Whatever has been going on?'

Clive felt safe enough to risk winding his window down an inch or so.

'Hello, Mrs Dominics. I'm sorry about your car. We didn't mean to drive into it.'

'Oh, don't worry about me,' she said. 'You've barely dented my bumper. It's your car that's come off the worst of it, I'm afraid. But never mind that for now. What's all this about diamonds and necklaces going missing? And Daphne Spurter? And your father being arrested? And all the rest? I only just heard this morning and I told Chaswick to bring me here immediately. Whatever is going on?'

'Oh, Mrs Dominics,' I said, feeling it was now safe to get out of the car, 'our dad's been framed and set up by person or persons unknown.'

'Tell her who they are,' Clive said.

'We don't know who they are!' I told him. 'I just said that. Though I have my suspicions.'

'But I don't understand, boys. Just tell me what happened. From the beginning. Did someone break into the hotel? And blow the safe? All I know is what I heard on the news.'

'No, Mrs Dominics, the safe was opened in the usual way. Whoever opened it knew the combination. And the only one in the hotel who knew it was our dad. Because you told it to him. Right?'

'That's right. I did.'

'So the police arrested him, as they thought he must have stolen the jewels. They said it was an inside job.'

'But your father would never steal anything . . .'

'We know. But the police don't. And once they'd arrested Dad, there was no one to look after us, so they were going to take us into Care—'

'And make us wear corduroy trousers,' Clive butted in. 'So we went on the run in a cardboard box and he was *Fragile* and I was *This Way Up*. But we realized that wasn't doing any good so we put Plan B into action and then Plan C – but don't ask me what Plan A was, because I don't remember seeing it.'

'But I don't understand,' Mrs Dominics said. 'The only two people who know the combination of the hotel safe are myself and your father. I certainly didn't take the gems. And I'm positive your father didn't . . .'

Yet even as Mrs Dominics said that, I could see the doubt in her eyes. In a way, I couldn't blame her either. Logically, she had to doubt our dad, because she knew *she* hadn't stolen the jewellery, and if Dad was the only other one able to open the safe . . .

'Mrs Dominics,' I said, 'there's someone else who knows the combination, isn't there?'

She looked at me.

'I don't think so. Who?'

'Mrs Dominics, you asked Dad to come and look after the hotel as acting manager, didn't you? What about the usual manager? Didn't he know the combination to the safe?'

'Well, yes,' she admitted. 'Of course. But he isn't here, you see, boys. He is away travelling, on a six-week tour of hotels around the world. He isn't even in the country.'

'Isn't he, Mrs Dominics?' I said. 'Are you sure

about that? All because he said he was going, that doesn't mean he went. Or maybe he did go, maybe he did. And he flew back, just for a few hours. That's all it would take.'

'But Mr Arbuthnot would never do . . .'

Then she trailed off, and she stood there, silent and lost in thought.

'I mean, Mr Arbuthnot – he's run the hotel for over two years . . .'

She looked at Chaswick, who looked back at her with the kind of look which seemed to speak volumes, and all the volumes said the same thing: I never fully trusted that Arbuthnot. I always felt uneasy about him.

'But Mr Arbuthnot came with the finest references,' Mrs Dominics said, as much to convince herself as anyone listening.

Forged, probably, Chaswick's expression appeared to say. Forged, I wouldn't be surprised. Playing the long game he was, biding his time, waiting for the big pay-off. Two years' work and more than five million quid's worth of gems at the end of it. Not a bad little pay day.

'He wouldn't even need to have done it himself,' I pointed out. 'He could have told the combination to an accomplice. There could have been two or three of them in it. And what better alibi for him – he was out of the country, thousands of miles away.'

'Exactly,' Clive said. 'It's like Mr Bun the Detective

said, Mrs Dominics. When you don't know who did it, then the only one who could have done it, is the one who didn't.'

'Well, I'm not sure about that, Clive, but—'

'I've got his address, Mrs Dominics,' I said. 'I've got Mr Arbuthnot's address. Right here.'

'However did you get that?'

'Plan C,' Clive said.

'We "borrowed" it from the filing cabinet in the manager's office.'

'He means he stole it, basically,' Clive said. 'I was only keeping a lookout. I'm prepared to testify against him if it means a definite conviction.'

'Well, if what you say is true, boys,' Mrs Dominics said, 'and your suspicions are correct, we must go to the police.'

Clive and I shared a nervous look. What if I was wrong? What if Mr Arbuthnot had had nothing to do with it? And we had to start again to find the real culprit? Well, we wouldn't be able to, not with the police involved. They'd not only have Dad in custody, they'd have us as well.

'Em, maybe it's best not to involve the police just yet, Mrs Dominics. Not until we're one hundred per cent sure. Just to be on the safe side.'

'I'd agree with that, ma'am,' Chaswick said – an unlikely and an unexpected ally to come to our aid. 'I think we should handle this ourselves for the moment. I can have a word with that Arbuthnot on your behalf, if you'd care for me to do so, ma'am.'

And Chaswick flexed his fingers and pulled his driving gloves up so that they were nice and tight. He did seem to have very big fists. They looked about the size of pumpkins.

'OK, boys,' Mrs Dominics said. 'Let us go and pay Mr Arbuthnot a visit – if he is in. Chaswick?'

I passed the paper I had taken from the manager's office over to him. He glanced at the address upon it.

'I can find it, ma'am,' he said. 'If you'd care to return to the car.'

'Boys?' Mrs Dominics said. 'I take it that you're also coming along?'

'Wouldn't miss it, Mrs Dominics,' I said, 'for the world. We'll just push our car out of the way.'

Which we did. Then we got into the back of Mrs Dominics's Rolls Royce and leant back into the soft, luxurious seats.

'Ah,' Clive sighed. 'This is the life, Mrs Dominics. This is more what I'm used to. I mean, I don't mind roughing it every now and again in a cardboard box, with a cup of soup from the soup run and a boiled-egg Buddhist sandwich, but this is the life for me. In fact, to be honest, I could get used to this.'

She looked at him and smiled a crinkly old smile.

'Yes, Clive,' she said. 'I'm sure you could.'

'But I'd rather do without all of it and sleep in a

box for ever,' Clive added, 'if it meant we could have Dad back . . .'

'I know, Clive,' she smiled. 'I know that too.'

'OK, well, drive on Chaswick, my man!' Clive instructed. 'Ride to the rescue. And don't spare the horses!'

I noticed the way Chaswick's driving gloves seemed to strain around the knuckles when he heard Clive say that. He gripped the steering wheel tightly and squeezed it hard, as if imagining that his fingers were clenched around something else, something more pliable.

Something like Clive's neck.

19

The House

'That must be it.'

The Rolls Royce pulled up the way Rolls Royces probably always pull up, gliding to a halt with a soft, barely audible *whoosh*.

'Hmm,' Mrs Dominics said. 'Doesn't look very promising, I'm afraid.'

We were parked in a quiet, deserted street, looking across at a white-painted, pebble-dashed house with green shutters.

When Mr Arbuthnot wasn't staying at the Hotel Royal, this was where he lived, in a rented, detached house, well out of London. It sat in its own grounds, surrounded by old oaks and willow trees, whose branches shielded it from prying eyes. He lived here alone. According to Mrs Dominics there was no Mrs Arbuthnot, nor any Arbuthnots junior.

'Married to his career, I always thought,' she said.

'Not the most approachable of men, but he came with good references. He was very well-organized and highly efficient.'

Yes, I thought, you'd have to be, if you were thinking of stealing five million dollars' worth of diamonds. You'd have to be organized, and you'd need a lot of patience too.

He must have waited for months for a chance like this to come up. He'd have known it was coming too. A guest like Daphne Spurter, with a big film premiere ahead of her, wouldn't have just turned up on the off-chance of getting a room – not with an entourage of hangers-on the size of hers.

She would have been booked in by the film studio well in advance, giving Mr Arbuthnot (and I was more and more convinced that he had done it, even though neither Clive nor I had as much as set eyes on him) plenty of time to ask Mrs Dominics for a nice, long, well-deserved six-week break so he could 'travel extensively and see how things are done in the other hotels. Have to keep abreast of the competition, Mrs Dominics, wouldn't you say?' It was the best possible alibi.

And of course, she'd have agreed. She'd have seen the good sense in it. She'd have thought of Mr Arbuthnot as a valuable, hard-working employee – which he no doubt had been so far, as that was the image he would have wished to create.

So Mrs Dominics would have looked around for a

temporary replacement – someone trustworthy, someone similarly well-organized and efficient, someone she'd like to give an opportunity to – like our dad.

And creepy, crooked Arbuthnot would have sat and waited in his house, while everyone thought he was away travelling, just biding his time, rubbing his hands with glee, knowing that Daphne Spurter would entrust her jewellery to the hotel safe. Then all Arbuthnot had to do was to enter the hotel, disguising himself as a waiter, or a porter, or to get some accomplice to do the dirty work for him, and open the safe in the small hours, when there was nobody about, take the diamonds and away.

Leaving our dad to get blamed for it.

That was what made me mad. That was the worst bit of all. It wasn't stealing the diamonds. To be honest, I didn't care if Daphne Spurter had all her diamonds stolen. They were no doubt all insured anyway, so she wouldn't really have been any the poorer in the long run.

No, it was the cold, calculating, creepy way that Arbuthnot had set somebody else up to take the blame for his dishonesty.

Five million dollars' worth of diamonds – our dad could get ten years inside for that. For Arbuthnot, Mrs Swanker Watson's jewellery would just have been an unexpected bonus.

'Ten years!' I'd said as much to Clive as we'd been driving along. 'Ten years inside!'

'We'll be grown up by the time he gets out,' Clive said. 'We'll have finished school and got jobs.'

In actual fact I didn't believe that Clive would be grown up, not even in ten years, and as for anyone ever giving him a job, it seemed highly unlikely to me. Most people wouldn't even have trusted Clive with a dustpan and brush.

But now that we were here, parked across the road from Mr Arbuthnot's house, my watertight theories and cunning deductions suddenly seemed leaky and not so clever after all.

'The house looks pretty much deserted to me, I'm afraid,' Mrs Dominics said. 'It does seem as if he's gone away. Look – the blinds are drawn upstairs, the shutters are closed on the ground floor. Why, there are even two pints of milk on the doorstep and a newspaper in the letterbox.'

I had to admit there was.

Only . . .

It was wrong.

People didn't do that when they went away. They didn't leave the place so obviously unoccupied, with old newspapers poking out of the letterbox and milk curdling on the step. That wasn't what they did at all. They tried to leave the place looking as though somebody was still at home. They stopped the papers, they cancelled the milk. They left the curtains open, with lights inside on timers, going on and off throughout the evening. They left the radio and the TV sets on timers too, so that there was the sound of voices and the flickering of the screen – so that from the outside everything seemed natural and normal and the same as ever.

That was what you did when you went away, and you did it in the hope of deterring any would-be burglars who might happen to be in the vicinity, searching for empty, easy-to-burgle houses.

So if you tried to make it look as if you were still there when in fact you had gone away, then it followed that if you tried to make it look as if you had gone away, it meant . . .

. . . you were still there.

'Mrs Dominics . . .'

But she wasn't listening, she was giving instructions to her chauffeur.

'I think that maybe we ought to just drive back to the hotel, Chaswick. I'm afraid, by the look of it, that we've come here on a wild goose chase.'

Chaswick started up the car and began to put it in gear.

'Mrs Dominics, no . . .' Clive said. 'You can't!'

'I'm sorry, boys. We all so want your father to be innocent, of course we do, but as you can see for yourselves, the house is quite deserted and—'

'Mrs Dominics, please, wait,' I begged her. 'It's wrong. It's all wrong. When you go away you make it look as if you're still at home. You don't leave milk on the step and papers on view. Do you? He's trying to make it look as if he's gone when he's actually still there!'

'Shall we return via the motorway, ma'am, or would you prefer the back roads?' Chaswick asked.

The car was already moving, we were edging away from the kerb.

Then we got a reprieve. 'Wait a moment, Chaswick.' Mrs Dominics held up her hand. 'You know something,' she said, 'I think the boys might have a point. Arbuthnot wasn't the careless sort. Quite the opposite, in fact. He'd never have forgotten to cancel his milk and newspapers. Let's just take a walk across the road and have a little look.'

'As you wish, ma'am,' Chaswick said through clenched teeth – it was plain that what Mrs Dominics wished wasn't what he wished at all. I think he would have been quite happy to see our dad in jail, and me and Clive along with him, whether we were innocent or not.

He parked the car again and stopped the engine.

'Right, boys,' Mrs Dominics said, reaching for the door. 'Let us go and see what we can see.'

'As you wish, ma'am,' Chaswick sighed. 'I'll remain here with the car, shall I, awaiting your imminent return?'

'No, Chaswick,' she said. 'You can come with us. If

things are indeed as the boys suspect, somebody large is going to come in useful.'

Reluctantly Chaswick prised himself out of the driver's seat and locked the car.

'Didn't you tell me once, Chaswick,' Mrs Dominics said, 'that you used to do a little amateur boxing when you were younger?'

'Only in the evenings, ma'am,' Chaswick said.

'Ah. Well, this might be an opportunity for you to do some during the day.'

So saying, she led the way across the road to the shuttered and apparently deserted house of Mr Terence Tarquin Arbuthnot, sometime hotel manager, and – if our suspicions were proved to be correct – long-term conman and professional jewel-thief.

'We'll go this way.'

Mrs Dominics, with Chaswick right behind her, pushed the garden gate open and went around to the left.

I was all set to follow them. But of course, Clive – being Clive – had to go the other way. Clive had to go to the right. The left wasn't good enough for him. Oh no. Clive has always had a contrary streak. If Clive was a lemming, he wouldn't follow the others off the cliff, no, he'd probably just stand there hiding behind a bush, watching them until they had all jumped off, then he'd sneak home and have a cup of tea or something. And if he was a Canadian goose, he wouldn't migrate south in the winter with all the others either – he'd just stay where he was and freeze to death for the sake of being different.

'Mrs Dominics!'

I said it in one of those 'loud whispers'. The kind you use when you need to shout but you don't want to be overheard – you sort of want to draw attention to yourself by remaining anonymous.

'Mrs Dominics! Chaswick! Hold on!'

They didn't hear my loud whisper and I didn't want to make it any louder in case it was heard inside the house. My instinct was that we should all stick together. But Clive was already off the other way, and I couldn't really leave him on his own – because at heart I'll probably always be the eldest and the responsible one – so I felt I had to go after him, if only to keep him out of trouble.

Not that anyone can really keep Clive out of trouble, for trouble is his natural element. You may as well try to keep frogs out of ponds, cats out of flaps, and cheese out of mousetraps.

'Clive!'

I caught up with him.

'What?'

'The other two have gone the other way!'

'Well, that's all right,' he said. 'They can circle round their way, we can circle round this way, and we'll meet round the back. Come on.'

The house was bigger than it had seemed from the road. It didn't actually face the road either. It was side on to it. The way Mrs Dominics and Chaswick had gone would take them to the front door; our way would lead us to the kitchen door, and then we should meet up again at the back.

'See anything?'

Clive was at one of the downstairs, shuttered windows. He'd trampled over the flowerbed to get to it.

'Clive,' I said. 'Mind the flowers.'

'They're weeds,' he said.

'How do you know?'

He pointed to a piece of paper pegged into the earth next to his foot.

'It says so on the packet.'

'Don't be stupid, Clive,' I said. 'Who's going to buy a packet of weed seed to plant in their flowerbeds?'

'Well, someone's got to plant them,' he said. 'They can't just come up from nowhere.'

I tiptoed carefully across the flowerbeds to join him.

'Well? See anything?'

'No, nothing.'

We peered in through the cracks in the shutter. All we could see was a dark, empty room, which looked like it could have been a study.

'Let's go on.'

We retraced our steps, past the packet with the word *Geraniums* on it.

'See,' Clive said. 'Geranium weeds.'

'Geraniums aren't weeds,' I told him.

'I bet a weed would think they were.'

'Come on.'

We came to another shuttered window; again we tried to peer inside; again we saw nothing but dark emptiness and unoccupied silence. But then . . .

'Listen!' Clive said.

'What?'

We stood, alert and attentive. After a few seconds, I heard it too.

'Voices. Maybe it's Mrs Dominics and Chaswick, round the other side of the house.'

'No, it's coming from inside,' Clive insisted.

'Let's go a bit further round.'

We crept on round the house, keeping low, in case someone should suddenly peer out of a window and see us – though the windows were all shuttered or had the curtains drawn.

'Here.'

It had to be the kitchen, by my calculations, and that was just what it was. There was a patio outside it and two doors, both shuttered, which, when opened, would have afforded a nice view of the garden.

We edged along the patio and crouched down. Then we put our faces to the window and peered through the cracks in the shutters.

'Voices!' Clive said.

'Shh! Listen!'

'Look!'

It was hard to make out, but we could just about see them. There were four people sitting around the kitchen table: one woman and three men. The ordinary ceiling lights were on and, in addition to those, there was an anglepoise lamp on the table which was being used to illuminate something bright and sparkling.

'Clive,' I whispered. 'Do you see who it is?'

'Yes,' he said. 'I recognize two of them – from the hotel.'

So did I. One was a woman – Miss Brinkly – one of the receptionists who worked in the hotel lobby, and the second was none other than Lester – the big, ugly-looking porter who had been so unpleasant to us on the day we had arrived.

'So they're in on it too.'

'And that one must be Arbuthnot,' I said. 'The one sitting at the head of the table.'

'Must be,' Clive nodded.

Somehow, he just looked the part of the hotel manager, as if it were a role he had played for so long that he couldn't stop playing it even after the curtain had come down and the audience had gone home.

'Looks like a right smoothie to me,' I said.

He did too. He was dressed in a white shirt and

dark suit, with just a flash of colour in his tie and a hint of gold in his cufflinks.

'So who's the other one?' Clive said. 'The one sitting by the lamp?'

The man was small and podgy, with a half-halo of hair left on an otherwise shiny bald head. He had a jeweller's eyeglass screwed into his right eye, and he was examining something that glittered under the glare of the lamp.

'He must be a fence,' I whispered.

Clive gave me one of his what-an-idiot looks.

'Fence?' he said. 'How can he be a fence? Fences are what you have in gardens to keep the neighbours out. He doesn't even look like a set of railings, never mind a fence.'

'Clive,' I said, 'don't show your ignorance. I mean, I know you've got a lot of it, but that's no reason to flash it about trying to make others jealous and wish they were as stupid as you. A fence is what you call a person who buys stolen goods.'

Clive looked at me through narrowed eyes.

'Why?' he said.

'How do I know?' I told him. 'It's just what they're called. You might as well ask why a sproggit is called a sproggit and why a balloon is called a balloon and why a stupid, cross-eyed half-wit with no more brains than a dead worm should be called a "Clive".'

Clive didn't say anything for half a minute. Then, 'Is that an insult?' he said.

'Shh!' I said. 'Watch.'

We turned back to the window.

The man with the eyeglass took it from his eye. He looked across the table at the one who had to be Arbuthnot. He shook his head.

'Not as good as I expected,' he said. 'I couldn't give you more than a half a million for it – if that.'

If Arbuthnot was disappointed, he didn't show it. He just gave a smile, like a man who knows that the bargaining has only just started.

'Come on now, Colin,' he said. 'We all know the jewels are worth far more than half a mil. Far more.'

'They're hot though,' the fence said. 'Red-hot.' And he shook his fingers as if he'd just touched a hotplate.

'They'll cool down,' Arbuthnot said. 'Give them time.'

'Have to be broken up too,' the fence said. 'I couldn't sell them like this. Too recognizable. That Daphne Spurter's had her mug and her sparklers on the front page of too many newspapers.'

'So you break them up and have them reset. They're still worth a fortune. They can be turned into rings, brooches, earrings, pendants, bracelets . . .'

'All right. I'll give you three-quarters. And that's my best offer.'

'Colin, Colin,' the seemingly unflappable Arbuthnot said. 'Please. Let's cut the comedy and be

261

sensible. We're good friends. We go a long way back . . .'

I turned to Clive.

'He's done it before then,' I whispered. 'I wonder how many other hotel guests he's robbed, and how many other people's dads he's fitted up for it.'

'But you're not the only dealer in the world, Colin,' Arbuthnot continued. 'There are others. And don't forget, this has to be split three ways . . .'

Miss Brinkly nodded and Lester grunted. They plainly weren't going to be done out of their shares, and they were there to see that they got a good price for them.

'OK then,' Colin sighed. 'I might be able to go up to one and a half. But I'll be robbing myself.'

'No need to do that, Col,' Arbuthnot said. 'We can do that for you.'

They all laughed. But it wasn't a nice sort of laugh. It was nasty and unpleasant, and I thought of our dad, still under arrest and being held on suspicion of stealing the very jewels that were lying there on the kitchen table, under the gleam of the lamp.

'Come on, Col,' Arbuthnot said. 'Look at them again. Screw that eyeglass back into your eye and I'm sure you'll realize they're worth twice what you're offering, at the very least.'

The fence grunted, but he did put the jeweller's glass back to his eye and take another look.

'Not too long a look, mind,' Arbuthnot said. 'I do have a plane to catch soon. Everyone thinks I'm abroad at the moment – and that's just where I intend to be. I flew away and then came back on a – "borrowed" passport, shall we call it? But I don't want to stay away too long. My company might be missed. Don't want anyone asking any difficult and probing questions, do we?'

Lester the porter opened his mouth to join in the conversation, but just as he did, there was a crash – a loud, knocked-over dustbin crash, followed by the sound of a spinning, galvanized lid as it rolled over concrete and settled to a halt.

'What the—'

All four of them were on their feet.

I turned to Clive.

'What did you do that for!'

'It wasn't me.'

And for once, that was true. The noise had come from the other side of the house. Mrs Dominics – or more likely, considering the size of him, Chaswick – had had a close encounter with a dustbin.

'Someone out there!' Arbuthnot said. 'Round at the back! Someone sneaking about. Get them!'

He and Lester were on their feet, heading for the front door. As they went, I saw Lester reach to his inside pocket, and something bright and silver flashed momentarily in his hand

'Clive!' I said. 'Did you see that? He's got a gun.'

'What do we do?' Clive said, his voice full of panic. 'What do we do?'

My every instinct was to run, but something else told me not to.

'Don't move,' I said. 'Stay where we are. Don't move an inch!'

But to be honest, I was petrified. I couldn't have moved if I'd wanted to.

20

Up the Pipe

There was silence. I listened out to hear the sound of running, of a struggle maybe, some kind of fight. Then I realized how ridiculous that was. Poor old Mrs Dominics was a feisty character and pretty nimble for her age, but there was no way she could leg it back to the Rolls Royce before Arbuthnot and his sidekicks were out of the door. There wouldn't be much that Chaswick could do to help her either – not with a gun pointed at him – or, worse, at her.

'What are they going to do?' Clive said. 'What if they come round here, to this side of the house?'

But they didn't.

We pressed our noses back to the window. Arbuthnot and Lester had returned. With them they had Chaswick and Mrs Dominics. Lester had the gun pointed at her.

'Sit down and don't try anything, or the old girl'll pay for it,' Lester said.

'Now, now, Lester,' Arbuthnot told him, 'let's be a little more polite to our honoured guests.'

'Sit down!' Lester said. He roughly pushed Chaswick into a chair. 'Get some rope. Old clothes line or something. Whatever there is,' he told Miss Brinkly.

She stood and went to look in an old-fashioned, walk-in larder. She found some twine in there and handed it to Lester. He tied Chaswick's hands behind him, around the back of the chair.

'I'll break your ******* neck when I get out of here,' Chaswick warned him. Then he remembered who was sitting next to him and apologized to Mrs Dominics. 'Excusing my language, ma'am,' he said.

'Not at all, Chaswick,' Mrs Dominics said. 'I quite agree with you. My sentiments precisely. They're a right bunch of ****s and no mistake.'

I was very surprised to learn that Mrs Dominics knew words like that.

'She got it from Gilbert Rimsey probably,' Clive whispered. 'He's a bad influence on the elderly.'

'And when I've finished with your neck,' Chaswick continued, 'I'll stuff your foot into your mouth and make you chew it till it's gone, and then . . .'

But we didn't hear what he'd do after that, as Arbuthnot took a large roll of gaffer tape from a drawer and used it to keep him quiet.

'Much better,' he said. Then he turned to Mrs Dominics. 'So terribly sorry you had to get involved in this, Mrs Dominics,' he apologized. 'But we shan't detain you long. We'll just finish our business here and then we'll be off. There won't be any need for you to see any of us ever again.'

'I wish I'd never clapped eyes on you in the first place,' she said, 'you underhand, deceitful, conniving little—'

Arbuthnot brandished the roll of gaffer tape at her.

'I'd prefer not to,' he said. 'But if I have to, I will.'

Mrs Dominics fell silent. She looked away from him, then down at her feet. She looked somehow inconsolable, betrayed by someone she had trusted, and she looked sad and incredibly old.

'We've got to do something!' Clive whispered to me. 'And quick.'

'I know. Only what?'

'Call the police.'

'We don't have a phone.'

'Then let's knock on the door and ask if we can use theirs.'

'Clive, don't be a—'

'I don't mean this house. I mean another – down the road somewhere . . .'

But I had my doubts. I didn't know if anyone would even let us use their phone. It seemed like a quiet neighbourhood. If elderly people saw Clive coming to the door, they'd probably have a stroke, or a heart attack, or think he was some kind of endangered species looking for a bag of soft fruit.

'We've got to ring nine-nine-nine,' Clive continued. 'Or they're going to get away!'

'At least Mrs Dominics knows that Dad didn't do it,' I pointed out. 'She's a witness to that now. They'll have to let him go.'

'I know. But what about Daphne Spurter's gems? That fence will be away with them. And what about Mrs Dominics and Chaswick? They might get hurt. And just think how grateful Daphne Spurter will be to get her jewels back. She might even reward the person who retrieved them—'

'With a big load of money, yeah, Clive! I didn't think of that!'

'With a kiss,' he said.

He had that smitten look on his face again, like he'd have lain down in a puddle and allowed Daphne Spurter to walk all over him, rather than let her get her feet wet.

'Clive,' I said, realizing that I would have to be cruel to be kind. 'You and Daphne Spurter, it's never going to be. It's a non-starter from the off. You've got nothing in common at all. She's about fifteen years older than you and she's rich, famous and beautiful. What have you got to match that?'

'I've got my collection of interestingly-shaped pencil stubs,' he said.

But I still couldn't see it working out, not even with Clive bringing his pencil stubs to the relationship.

Before I could elaborate further on the futility of his crush on Daphne Spurter, I realized that Clive had stepped away from the shuttered window and was gazing up at the roof.

'What?' I said. 'What are you thinking of?'

'The phone,' he said. 'A house this size, there'll be phones everywhere. In all the bedrooms probably. We could ring the police on one of them.'

'But we can't get in, Clive. Everything's locked and shuttered. And we daren't break anything, they'll hear us.'

'No,' he said. 'There *is* a way. I can see it from here.'

'What?'

'Easy. Up the drainpipe . . .'

'Yes?'

'And down the chimney.'

I raised my hand to my eyes, sheltering them from the light.

Clive was right. The house was old and the chimneys were of the same vintage – they were wide and oblong, looking like the kind of chimneys that sweepers once cleaned by sending small boys down them, back in the bad old days, like in *The Water Babies*.

'We'll get filthy dirty,' I said.

'Doesn't frighten me,' Clive said. Which was true of course. A bit of dirt had never frightened Clive, ever. It was the soap he was afraid of.

Having had experience of shinning up drainpipes with Clive before, I decided to wait a bit, until he was well on his way. Clive has a tendency to put his foot on the head of the person beneath him when he is shinning up drainpipes, so it is a good idea to leave a gap between yourself and him.

Although the house was old, the drainpipes were in good condition. They were the heavy cast-iron ones too; had they been flimsy, plastic ones, they'd never have held our weight.

I decided not to look down as we climbed, for heights make me dizzy. But I couldn't look up either, because that way was an even more terrifying prospect – a view of Clive and his bum. I just stared at the wall and kept climbing, until finally I reached the gutter.

'Up here,' Clive said from above me. 'It's all right as long as you don't look down.'

Of course, him saying that made me look down, to see why I shouldn't.

I nearly passed out. The house hadn't looked that high when we had been down at the bottom, in the garden. But now that we were up at the top, the patio seemed about two miles away. I started to wobble and grabbed out for something to hold on to as I clambered over the valley gutter and onto the roof.

'Let go of my leg!' Clive said.

'Not until I'm safely over,' I told him.

I rolled over the parapet and onto the valley gutter.

'That was fun, eh, wasn't it?' Clive said.

'Yes,' I said. 'Hilarious. I've not enjoyed myself so much since I fell off my bike and got concussion.'

'Ah, yes,' he said. 'I remember. I enjoyed that too when you did that. Come on then, let's get to the chimney.'

There was a cluster of them, of four, wide, gaping-mouthed chimneys. At the other end of the roof were another four. We climbed up and peered down each one in turn.

'Well?'

'All look pretty dark to me, Clive,' I said. 'Maybe this isn't such a—'

'Which one then?' he said. 'Which do you fancy?'

I didn't fancy any of them. 'I dunno,' I said. 'How can we tell where any chimney comes out? One of them might come out in the kitchen, for all we know. If we go down that, we're straight out of the frying pan.'

'How about you go down one, I'll go down another one. Then that doubles our chances.'

There was some truth in that, but I was worried that something might go wrong, and there one us would be, stuck at the bottom of a chimney on his own. Whereas if we went down together, even if things didn't work out, I'd always be able to eat Clive if necessary and so increase my chances of survival.

'Put your ear to each one, listen for their voices. If you hear them, then that one'll be the kitchen chimney. And keep your voice low, or *they* might hear *us*.'

We listened at each of the chimneys.

'That one,' I mouthed, pointing at one from which faint, murmured conversation had emerged. 'That's the kitchen down there.'

Clive nodded.

'So let's go down this one,' he mouthed back, pointing to one of the other stacks.

'OK,' I whispered. 'After you.'

I thought it would be best if Clive went first, then I would have something to land on.

'Cor, I get to go first, do I?' Clive said, thinking that this was an honour.

'That's it, Clive. Off you go. I'll give you half a minute before I follow, and I'll see you at the bottom.'

'I don't suppose you'd have a torch on you, would you?'

'No, I wouldn't, Clive. I didn't actually know when we set off that we'd be doing Santa Claus impressions when we got here.'

'OK then. Here goes. If Father Christmas can do it with a sack of presents and a reindeer under his arm, then so can we. Do you think there'll be any mince pies down there?'

He clambered up and sat on the edge of the stack, his legs dangling into the mouth of the chimney.

'It does look very dark,' he said.

'Well take it easy, Clive,' I said. 'Just a bit at a time. Don't try and slide down the whole thing at—'

'Geronimo!' Clive said, and he was gone.

'. . . at once.'

His disappearance was shortly followed by a sack-of-potatoes-landing-in-a-fireplace kind of noise.

'Clive!' I whispered down the chimney. 'Are you all right?'

A tremulous, echoing voice replied from the depths and the darkness.

'I think so – only . . .'

'I'm coming down,' I said. 'Here I come.'

I edged my way over the lip of the chimney and started to walk my way down, wedging an arm here and a leg there.

Finally I felt something beneath me. Something moving. Something alive.

'Ahh – what is it?'

'You're standing on my head,' Clive said.

I managed to slide down beside him. I reached out and felt around. My hands made contact with something clammy, damp, and weirdly repulsive.

'Clive, is that you?'

'Of course it's me. And get your finger out of my eyeball. Who else would it be? Who else would you expect to meet at the bottom of a chimney?'

'I don't know – Clive . . .'

'What?'

'I can't see anything.'

'Neither can I. It's totally black. It's so black in here it's practically white.'

I looked up. The only light I could see was way back up at the top of the chimney.

'Clive, there should be some light – coming from the fireplace . . . Where's the fireplace, Clive?'

'I dunno. I've not been here before. I don't go down chimneys that much. I'm more the outdoors type.'

'Clive – if there's no light visible, then they must have bricked the fireplace up.'

'What!'

'Bricked it up. And we can't get out. And we'll never be able to climb back up again and—'

'You mean – we're – we're –'

'Yes, I do,' I said. My heart was pounding. My mouth was dry. The worst of my terrors had become reality. 'We're buried alive, bricked up in a chimney, and no one knows we're here – first the thirst will come . . . then the hunger . . . then we'll go mad . . . and then . . . we'll die.'

'Oh dear,' Clive said. 'In that case – I mean, I

don't suppose you brought a pack of playing cards, did you, to give us something to do while we're going mad?'

'No I did not! And how would we be able to see them anyway?'

'No, that's right. We wouldn't be able to see them, would we?' Clive said, in a really sarcastic voice. 'And why wouldn't we able to see them? Because Mr Incompetence here didn't just forget the playing cards to pass the time while we were going mad, he forgot the torch as well. So not only do we have to go mad, we have to go mad in the dark. Absolutely typical. And people say that I'm disorganized. Huh!'

'Look, Clive,' I said, 'I might not be able to see you, but I can hear you, and I'm pretty sure I can get my hands round your windpipe, even in the dark, and there won't be any witnesses and—'

'Hang on,' he said. 'Listen.'

He had kicked against something with his foot. There was a hollow sound – not the sound of solid brick, but the empty sound of plywood or plasterboard.

'It's all right,' he said. 'They haven't bricked the fireplace up. It's just wood or plaster or something. Let's give it a shove.'

The two of us kicked and pressed against it. The panel soon gave, collapsing forwards, and we rolled out from the chimney to find ourselves in a bedroom – a large, airy, spacious bedroom.

With beautiful white carpets.

'Flipping heck!'

'What are you staring at?' Clive said.

'You,' I said. 'You look like a lump of coal.'

'Well, what do you think you look like? You look like a charcoal brick. We could have a barbecue.'

Clive went to look at himself in the full-length mirror in the wardrobe. He was completely covered in soot. His clothes were black, his hair was black, and as he walked little puffs of black powder fell from him.

'Clive! The carpet!'

There were big, black footprints on it – a trail of them, leading from the chimney.

'Can't worry about that now,' he said. 'Where's the phone?'

'By the bed. Only don't sit—'

Too late. He sat down on the beautiful white bedspread.

'Oh dear,' he said. Then, 'Not to worry. It'll wash out.'

'The phone, Clive – come on, come on!'

I tiptoed over to join him. Why I was tiptoing, I didn't really know. I somehow felt I'd leave smaller footprints on the carpet.

'What's the number again?' he said. 'Of the emergency services? It's three-three-three, isn't it?'

'No. It's nine-nine-nine.'

'Well, I was half right.'

'Look, Clive, give the phone to me!'

'I'm doing it!'

He dialled nine-nine-nine.

'Hello,' he whispered into the phone. 'Yes, I want the police. Thank you. Hello. Listen. It's Clive here. I've just come down the chimney and we've got an emergency on our hands. I'm here with my brother, who's covered in soot. We had to kick a hole in the fireplace and there aren't any mince pies. How Santa Claus manages it, I can't imagine. You'd think he'd get his sack stuck. Anyway, the thing is, Mrs Dominics and Chaswick are tied up downstairs and they've also got the diamonds. Can you get round here as soon as possible? Oh, and we're sorry about the carpets.'

There was a pause.

'What're they saying?' I asked.

'She's saying do I know what the penalty for hoax phone calls and wasting police time is?'

'Tell her it's real! Give me the phone!'

I snatched it from him.

'Hey! I was doing that!'

'Be quiet, Clive. This is serious.' I spoke into the mouthpiece. 'Hello. This is Clive's brother. I know he sounds like a half-wit, but it's true. It's the people who stole Daphne Spurter's diamonds. They've got them, right here. And they're leaving, any minute, for the airport. Sorry? What did you say? Where? Where are we, you mean? The address?'

I looked at Clive.

'Clive. Where are we? What's the address of this place?'

'I dunno. I just came here in the car.'

Then I remembered I had it on the paper, the one I'd taken from the manager's office. I'd given it to Chaswick, then he'd given it back – I thought – or had he?

'Hang on a moment, I'll find the address – I've got it here—'

But before I could, I looked up to see myself staring down the barrel of what looked like a real gun with real bullets in it.

It was Lester. The nasty porter from the hotel. He must have heard the noise when we kicked out the panel covering the fireplace, and had come up to investigate. He looked even nastier and uglier out of uniform than he did in it.

'I'll take that.'

He snatched the telephone and spoke into it.

'Sorry about that. My kids got hold of the phone. Messing about. I do apologize. Thank you. Not at all.'

And he replaced the handset onto its cradle.

'Well, well,' he said. 'What have we got here? It's a lump of coal and an ashtray. Won't you come and join us, boys, in the kitchen?' He beckoned with the gun. 'Move it!'

We had no choice than to do as he said. So we

walked towards the door and out onto the landing, leaving black, sooty footprints behind us.

Mrs Dominics was tied up, next to Chaswick, and in a few minutes, so were we.

'Nice and tight,' Arbuthnot said. 'We don't want them squirming out of it until we're well and truly gone.'

'*Ummpa . . . ohhpa . . . drumpaaa . . . chunrnka . . .*' Clive said, from behind the piece of gaffer tape which had been wound around his mouth.

It was funny, I had never really thought much about gaffer tape before, but now that Clive had some stuck on his gob, I was beginning to see its merits.

Or I was until I got some around my mouth too.

'Right,' Arbuthnot said. 'Lovely job. We'll be off then. You shouldn't be here for too long. Just a few days. Then once we're safely landed in South America – not that it will be South America, of course, because I'm not really going to tell you where we're going, am I? – but let's call it South America for now – and it might well even be South America – but that's not your concern – anyway, we'll ring someone up to let them know where you are, once we're safely landed and well out of reach of any authorities here.'

'*Greshca . . . ooda . . . beeda . . . beeda . . . chk!*' Chaswick mumbled from behind his gag. I think it was probably some kind of threat.

'So you shouldn't be stuck here for more than a couple of days. Three at the most. Certainly no more than four,' Arbuthnot said.

Four?

Four days, tied to a chair, with no food or drink, and not able to go to the toilet? I didn't think Mrs Dominics would survive four days. I didn't think she'd survive one.

'Or then again,' he continued, 'we might just all get an attack of collective amnesia, and forget to tell anyone about you at all.'

Lester seemed to think the idea of forgetting all about us to be immensely funny. He chuckled to himself, in a deep, throaty laugh.

They were packing up now, ready to leave. They seemed to have agreed on a price for the diamonds. It was just a matter of picking up the money and dividing it between them. Then the fence would have the jewels and they would all be away.

Leaving us tied and trussed up in the kitchen, with nobody knowing where we were, hoping that somebody would find us.

Only what if they never did?

'Just check through the house,' Arbuthnot said to the others, who were ready to go. 'Make sure that nothing incriminating's been left lying around. Only take a few minutes.'

He'd have got away if it hadn't been for that. They

all would. Life – as Dad is fond of saying – is full of little ironies. Yes, if Arbuthnot hadn't bothered to make sure that they wouldn't get caught, then they probably never would have been caught.

And we might still be trussed up in the kitchen.

Skeletons by now.

It probably took him seven or eight minutes to check through the house, all the way from top to bottom.

'You two made a right mess of my bedroom, didn't you?' he said, when he returned to the kitchen. 'But never mind. Not my problem now.' He turned to the others. 'OK then,' he said. 'Let's go. And Lester . . .'

'What?'

'Put that gun away. We can't walk out into the street with a gun. We're innocent, law-abiding citizens now, remember. In fact it might be better if you got rid of it. Wipe your prints off it and wrap it in a bag. We'll lose it on the way.'

He did as Arbuthnot said. They took a last look around the kitchen and then headed for the door.

I think they must have got quite a surprise when they opened it.

There were five policemen at the front door.

And another ten around the back.

We hadn't been able to give them the address before Lester had nabbed us, but they'd traced it from the phone number.

The lady who had answered the nine-nine-nine

call had done something which few people who have had a telephone conversation with Clive have done ever.

She had actually taken him seriously.

21

And Home . . .

'I suppose,' Clive said, as he sat half hidden behind his ice-cream sundae in the Hotel Royal Grill, 'that after a while you get used to saving the day and being a hero and stuff like that. Personally, I take all that sort of thing in my stride now and I don't let it go to my head. I just regard it as all in a day's work and I don't look for honours and knighthoods and recognition and certificates with *Well Done, Clive* written on them. To me, doing good is its own reward.'

We weren't the only ones at the table. There was Dad, Mrs Dominics, even Chaswick, who'd been let out of his chauffeur's uniform for the evening to join the celebrations, along with various other friends and well-wishers, including Mr and Mrs Swanker Watson and Swanker himself.

'Look, Clive,' I said. 'You didn't save the day at all.

If anyone did any day-saving, it was me. If it hadn't been for my quick thinking and hair-trigger reflexes, not to mention my methods, plans, and my Sherlock-Holmes-like famous deductions, you'd still be tied to a chair with two metres of gaffer tape round your gob – and no bad thing either, some might say.'

'You,' Clive said, 'are just jealous. It was me who thought of going down the chimney.'

'Yeah, and I'd have thought of something better,' I said, 'that didn't involve getting a sack of soot up your nose and ten kilos of muck down your underpants. But then, Clive, I guess that ten kilos of muck down your pants is pretty much a good-pants day for you. I only agreed to the chimney ploy so as to let you have things your way for once, just to keep your pecker up and so you wouldn't feel like a total loser all your life. I had all sorts of alternative schemes at my disposal, I just decided not to bother with them.'

'Good ice-cream this,' Swanker Watson said, shovelling in more, along with half a banana and some cream.

Everybody seemed to be enjoying themselves, even Mrs Swanker Watson, who is normally only known for long faces and finding faults and problems where none existed before. Though plainly this did not apply to Mr Swanker Watson, who had been nothing but faults for a long time.

I noticed that she was wearing her jewellery. The police had returned it to her, and there she was, sparkling like a polished window. She was quite the centre of attention, which she didn't seem to object to.

'Yes, this is the life,' Clive went on, getting more boastful by the second. I started to eye up the ice-bucket, wondering if it would fit over his head. 'First the danger and hardships, then the ice-cream and the glory. That's how I like it. In fact, when I grow up, I might join MI6 or the MI5 or whatever it is and be a James Bond sort of bloke, licensed to do cooking and stuff.'

'No, Clive,' I corrected him. 'James Bond is licensed to kill. Not licensed to grill.'

'Whatever,' Clive said dismissively. 'But that's who I'm going to be. Or I might become a detective and be Clive of the Yard.'

'The only yard anyone would let you be a Clive of would be a builder's yard – they'd let you sweep it with a broom.'

But he wasn't listening.

'Yes,' he said. 'I shall wear a tuxedo and drink milk – shaken, not stirred – and I shall save ladies from perils and dangers and ride a mountain bike with personalized number plates and – and – and . . .'

Then he went a bright red colour and suddenly became all awkward and tongue-tied. I glanced up to see what he was looking at and why he had suddenly gone so bashful.

I saw and heard simultaneously.

A strong American accent was wafting across the room, and following it was Daphne Spurter, with her mega-million-dollar necklace around her neck – and she looked like another million all on her own. Trying to keep up with her was the full entourage.

'Where are they?!' she was saying. 'I gotta see them. I gotta thank these guys in person.'

She was heading for our table.

Clive, meanwhile, was trying to hide under it.

'Excuse me,' Daphne Spurter said, stopping at the head of the table, next to Dad. 'Mr Johnson, I believe I have something to thank you for – and your two boys.'

Clive was now beetroot-coloured. Pickled beetroot-coloured.

'Where are they? I must thank them in person.'

'Really, Miss Spurter,' Dad said. 'It's I who should thank you for taking all this so well. And I can only apologize for—'

'Apologize?' she said. 'No apology needed, Mr Johnson. Now where are those boys?'

She bore down upon us as only a movie star can, while Clive sat there like a pussy-cat in the headlights, knowing that the lorry was coming for him, but unable to get out of its way.

'Oh you guys!' Daphne Spurter said. 'There you

are! And you're the ones who rescued my jewels!'

'Eh, not me, actually,' Swanker Watson said. 'I'm only here for the banoffee pie and the after-dinner mints.'

Daphne Spurter swept him away with a gesture. It was as if she really had made him disappear.

'Then you guys,' she said. 'You're the two I have to thank. Here, boys, now there's a little something for you . . .'

She pressed some banknotes into both our hands.

'And here's a little something else from me, something real personal, something I want you never to forget, something I want you to remember when you're grown and your daddy's age. You'll be able to tell your grandchildren . . .'

Clive was all but under the table. He could see it coming, and part of him wanted to get away from it –

'. . . that you once were . . .'

And yet another part of him –

'. . . kissed . . .'

Didn't –

'. . . by Daphne Spurter, from Hollywood.'

She laid one on me first. It was only on the cheek. But I got a sort of tingle. You could tell she was a movie star.

Then she headed for Clive. He'd gone completely dopey. In fact he looked a bit like a hamster, bracing itself for a kick up the backside.

'Thank you,' Daphne Spurter said. And she kissed him on the cheek too. 'Thank you – Clive.'

And Clive slowly and gently – and not without a certain style – fainted under the table.

'I'm never going to wash my face again,' Clive said, as he tried to get even more stuff into his suitcase.

'What do you mean *again*?' I said. 'You've yet to wash it in the first place.'

'She kissed me,' he said (for about the ten thousandth time) and going all moony again. 'She kissed me and called me Clive and said she'd wait for me, until I was grown up.'

'No she didn't, Clive.'

'She did. I heard her as I fainted.'

'No, Clive, she never said she'd wait for you until you'd grown up. She shouted to the waiter and said, "Waiter, I think this boy may have thrown up.'

'She didn't!'

'Who was conscious? Me or you?'

'Hey, you two – could you get on with the packing and keep the noise down a little?'

'Sorry, Dad.'

'Sorry.'

We were back in the penthouse suite. Our six weeks were over. It was time to go home. Mrs Dominics had come to see us off. Though in truth, she had also come to try and persuade Dad to stay.

'Won't you reconsider, John?' she said. 'You've

managed the place so well. Won't you consider it as a full-time appointment? You can all stay on here, in the penthouse suite, and the boys can go to school in London . . .'

We fell silent, wondering what he would say.

'Mrs Dominics,' Dad said. 'It's a wonderful offer, a marvellous one. And in some ways, I'd love to take it up – but in others . . .' He looked towards us and he lowered his voice a little. 'But in others – well, home is home, you know . . . and I travelled so much when I worked on the cruise liners . . . and I'd have to uproot the boys from their friends and their school and, well, their memories . . .'

When he said that, I couldn't help but think of Mum. And I thought it wouldn't be very nice if we were a long way away and couldn't go to the cemetery by the old church and take her flowers any more.

'I quite understand, John – I quite understand. And you do manage The Stowaway restaurant so well.'

'I can stay there?'

'Of course. And I'll find another manager for here. But if you ever change your mind . . .'

'Thank you, Mrs Dominics. But I don't think I will.' Then he called to us. 'Boys,' he said, 'we'd maybe better say goodbye to Mrs Dominics now.'

So we did.

We said goodbye to her and to everyone, to the

waiters and the maids and everyone we had got to know. Daphne Spurter had already gone by then, so we couldn't say goodbye to her.

Then we went out to the car park where our mostly repaired car (but still with the big dent in the front) waited for us.

Mrs Dominics and Chaswick were there to wave us off. We put our heads out of the window and yelled goodbye.

'Bye, Chaswick! Bye, Mrs Dominics!'

Then, in a quieter voice, as we drove along, I heard Clive say, 'Bye, London. Bye, Hotel Royal. Bye, adventures. Bye, excitement. Bye, kisses from Hollywood film stars. Bye, cardboard box marked *This Way Up*. Bye. Good bye. I don't suppose we'll ever meet again. Good bye.'

And somehow, for some reason, I felt a bit sad.

We were all pretty quiet on the long drive home. It was school again on Monday, and all the usual things and all the old routines. Clive looked a bit down, and I felt a bit sorry for him, because he was my brother, after all.

'Clive,' I said. 'You remember Plan C?'

'Plan C?'

'About how we were going to get into the manager's office and find Mrs Dominics's address?'

'Oh yeah. Your Plan C, about pretending to be bell-hops—'

'Clive,' I said. 'It wasn't my Plan C. I didn't have a Plan C. It was yours.'

He turned and looked at me, vaguely astonished.

'Was it?' he said.

'Yes,' I said. 'Credit where it's due, Clive. I didn't have a clue how we were going to do it. You thought of it. It was all yours.'

'So you mean . . .' Clive said. 'That I'm not stupid after all?'

'Apparently not,' I said. 'At least not as stupid as we'd thought.'

'Cor,' Clive said, brightening up no end. 'Plan C. Imagine that! And that was mine. Hey. That's not bad, is it? That's pretty good.'

I looked up and caught Dad's eye in the rear-view mirror.

I realized that he was smiling.

'All right, in the back?' he said.

'Fine, Dad,' I said.

'Fine, Dad,' Clive agreed.

'Home soon,' he said.

'Yeah. Home soon.'

'It's nice to go places,' he said. 'But it's always good to come home.'

And I could see there was something in that. I really could.

The familiar landmarks came into view: the streets, the hills, the houses, the river running down to the sea, the big liners moored to their capstans, the high cranes standing ready to unload the great cargo vessels and huge container ships.

'It's good to be back,' he said. 'And smell the sea.'

Then we turned another corner and there was our house, waiting for us.

'Hey Clive,' I said, as we pulled up in the drive. 'I don't really mind if you want to be the eldest for a while.'

He thought for a moment.

'Maybe we could take it in turns,' he said. 'You could be the eldest one week, and I could be the eldest the next.'

'Sounds all right to me,' I said.

So that was what we did.

Dad stopped the car. I remembered when we were really little and how he would pick us up and carry us in, both together, one in each arm.

But those days had gone now – as all days go.

I undid my seatbelt and told Clive I'd be in the house before him.

'You ******* won't!' he said, and we scrambled for the doors.

'Clive!' Dad said. 'Where on earth did you ever hear language like that?'

'At the Hotel Royal,' Clive told him.

'Well, don't use it here.'

I got to the house just before Clive did. But he said that he had got there first.

Dad gave this long, loud, exasperated sigh, and

said, 'Will you two ever stop arguing?!'

Though I think he already knew the answer to that one.

'Come on, Dad,' Clive said to him. 'I need the loo!'

Dad turned the key in the door lock. Clive pushed the door open and pounded up the stairs. And there we were. We were home. With the envelopes lying on the mat.

Sometimes I think that the future is like that. It's an envelope you haven't opened yet. But the letter inside is already written. It might even have news of some adventures in it.

'Let's see what the post has brought us then, while we've been away,' Dad said.

He tore the first of the letters open.

I wondered what it might contain.